"One rose for each day I've known you."

Hillary read the card. She knew she should be delighted by the sight of twenty-eight red roses. Instead, her jaw dropped.

Paul grasped one of her hands. "Your skin is like the petals on those roses."

This was turning into a paint-by-numbers romance! And Hillary didn't know what to do; it was all so hokey and embarrassing.

Paul released her hand and reached into his breast pocket to withdraw two airline tickets. "Come away with me."

Hillary grabbed her water glass, but there wasn't any water, only champagne. She couldn't speak. She couldn't even look at him.

Paul made a small sound. Now she looked at him. He was laughing at her! He must ha̶v̶e̶ h̶e̶a̶rd her talking about his "classic text̶b̶o̶o̶k̶ ̶r̶o̶m̶a̶n̶ce," and then staged this whole sc̶e̶n̶e̶ ̶a̶s̶ ̶a̶n̶ elaborate joke!

Heather Allison, who lives with her husband and two young sons in Houston, Texas, used to write letters, which she describes as ''hysterical sagas,'' to family and friends when she was in college--letters they enjoyed enough to share with complete strangers! She began to hear, ''You ought to write a book.'' So eventually, she did—*Deck the Halls,* her first Harlequin Romance. Then she wrote a second one, *Pulse Points.* And now she's working on a third. . . .

Books by Heather Allison

HARLEQUIN ROMANCE
3091—DECK THE HALLS

PULSE POINTS

Heather Allison

Harlequin Books

TORONTO • NEW YORK • LONDON
AMSTERDAM • PARIS • SYDNEY • HAMBURG
STOCKHOLM • ATHENS • TOKYO • MILAN

ISBN 0-373-03157-2

Harlequin Romance first edition November 1991

To Andy, Collin and Brett,
the men in my life

Special thanks to the emotional Pat Kay, the goal-
oriented Alaina Richardson, the logical Elaine
Kimberley, the lyrical Betty Gyenes and the slow-
down-it's-not-a-train-wreck Susan Brown.

PULSE POINTS

CHAPTER ONE

"I'M LOOKING FOR Hillary Simpson."

The voice was a deep bass, with the barest hint of an indefinable accent.

Hillary stopped packing bottles and turned to perform the deep curtsy required of her as the Renaissance Festival's perfumer.

But the man who stood in the doorway of her cottage was no ordinary festival patron. Dark charcoal slacks, topped by a crisp white shirt that hadn't wilted in Texas's October heat made him conspicuously overdressed, even though he had discarded the jacket and tie. Hillary surveyed the open collar of his shirt, and the black hair it revealed, then realized his brown eyes were making an equal appraisal of her costume's décolletage.

"I'm Mistress Simpson, m'lord." She belatedly sank to the dirt floor in a billow of crimson velvet.

Silence. The sun streamed through the dirty pseudo-Renaissance windows, making the little cottage an oven. Sweat trickled between Hillary's shoulder blades under her heavy red velvet costume.

Knees registering a silent protest, Hillary rose to her feet, trying not to trip over her full skirts. "How may I serve—" She broke off as she met the blazing fury in the handsome stranger's eyes. Eyes that had blazed with appreciation until he learned her identity.

Had someone complained that she'd closed her booth early? People hadn't exactly been crowding into her shop to purchase her expensive perfumes, although whenever she glanced through the connecting door she could see a steady stream of customers buying her partner's natural lotions and cosmetics. She nodded toward the rough-hewn table where her own rows of crystal bottles filled with amber liquid gleamed in the late-afternoon sun. "Would you care to sample some of my perfumes, m'lord? Or I can create a scent just for you. Something to remind m'lord of this day, perhaps?"

"I'll never forget this day." The man flicked a glance around the crude interior of the cottage before ducking to enter through the arched doorway. "I'm Paul St. Steven." He paused as if expecting a reaction.

He must assume she recognized his name. Her partner Melody Anderson might have, because she came here every weekend the festival was open. He was probably a fair official, about to reprimand Hillary for closing her booth.

She offered him her hand to shake. He took it at once, accompanying the social gesture with a social smile.

The smile improved an already attractive face. He had a generous mouth and nose, which looked exactly right for his molded cheeks and jaw. Nothing dainty about him. Just good and solid—and she didn't want him to be angry anymore. "I can explain," she said impulsively.

"Please do."

"The sun is bad for the perfumes. You wouldn't want me to sell inferior products at your festival, would you?"

"No." He paused briefly. "But this isn't my festival."

Hillary laughed. "I know, the *people's* festival." She reached out and touched him lightly on the arm. He tensed immediately. Hillary was a toucher, but she acknowledged that some people were not. This man was one of those. Too bad.

"Do you know who I am?" He raised his head slightly, with unconscious pride.

"One of the board members of the Renaissance Festival?"

"No."

"Oh." Then he wasn't here to reprimand her. "Oh," she said again, with audible relief and a smile.

Full lips pressed tightly together. He didn't smile back. Why was he so angry—and getting angrier?

"Where are the others?"

"What others?"

His eyes never leaving her face, his movements quick and controlled, Paul reached into his pocket and withdrew a piece of paper, unfolded it and held it in front of Hillary's face. "The other perfumers?"

Her eyes focused on a page torn from a magazine. *Hillary Simpson, owner of Scentsations in Buffalo Bayou Mall, Houston, Texas, announces an Independent Perfumers' Seminar...*

"Oh." Hillary knew the rest. A lump formed in her throat. She swallowed and felt the lump lodge halfway to her stomach. She'd been forced to postpone the seminar. Unfortunately the announcement had appeared in an issue of *Perfumer's Quarterly,* anyway. That meant this Paul was.... Surely not. Not after all the phone calls. Please not. "Are you St. Etienne's representative?"

"Then I am expected." His lips curved in a brief smile.

"What are you doing here? We're a two-hour drive from Houston." Alarm sharpened Hillary's voice. "I mean, this is the Renaissance Festival." She clutched her skirts and spread them out, even though he couldn't possibly have failed to notice her costume.

"You are holding your seminar here?" Paul indicated the festival grounds outside the cottage where a nine-foot ogre, with matted red-and-green hair, blew into a battered horn, attracting a crowd.

By now he knew perfectly well there was no seminar, Hillary thought. He was forcing her to play it out. "The seminar was canceled some time ago." Another trickle of sweat. How did his shirt manage to stay crisp and dry?

"Couldn't you be bothered to inform me?" His deep voice was cool—the only thing in the booth that was.

Hillary tried to retain an air of calm professionalism. The House of St. Etienne, dinosaur though it was, was still highly respected. It was one of the few French designer fashion houses with an in-house perfumer. Most other houses commissioned their perfumes from chemical companies and fragrance labs.

But St. Etienne was old guard, old wealth—and apparently old communications systems. "I did try to contact you." Hillary smiled sweetly. "I left messages with several people on two continents and had you paged for twenty-four hours at Kennedy airport—difficult since no one would tell me your name. No one would release your itinerary. No one would connect me with a secretary or your superior, and no one would speak anything but French!"

She bit off the last word, leaving her lower lip in a slight pout.

Paul's eyes seemed drawn to it. "And do you speak French?" he asked lightly.

"I speak some American French."

"Ah." Paul bowed his head, finger against his lips, and regarded Hillary's petite figure in the soggy red velvet. "I don't believe anyone in my office speaks American French."

"They should. Don't they want you to get your messages?"

"Perhaps my staff has been . . . overzealous in guarding my privacy."

"What are they guarding it from?"

Paul blinked, then straightened. "Please explain this." He dangled the magazine notice in front of her again.

"I wanted to reserve advertising space and sent a deposit with an ad for the summer issue. *Perfumer's Quarterly* ran the announcement in the spring issue, instead. I didn't have all the seminar details nailed down or hotel confirmation—"

"You should have reserved a hotel at least a year in advance!" Paul interrupted.

"A year ago, I hadn't thought of holding a seminar." A year ago she'd had no idea of what she was getting into. She'd thought sponsoring a seminar had been an inspired way to make her name known throughout the industry. Drat *Perfumer's Quarterly,* anyway. If their advertising department hadn't made the mistake, she would have been able to discreetly withdraw her notice, instead of enduring weeks of embarrassment as she responded to requests for information.

Hillary experienced a pang of regret. If she'd known that one of the most prestigious French fashion houses intended to send a representative, it might have saved the seminar.

"You were working alone?"

"Except for my partner, yes." Hillary raised her chin. Paul was taller than she—almost everyone was—but not so tall that her neck hurt when she looked up at him.

"That explains it, then." Paul nodded, as if to himself.

"Explains what?" Hillary already felt defensive, but she wasn't going to allow herself to be insulted, and she felt an insult coming.

"You . . . obviously do not have the ability to hold a seminar of any sort." He spoke dispassionately.

Hillary wished for instant height, a deeper voice, *straight* blond—wait, brunette—hair, no freckles and no dimples. While she was at it, she wished for different clothes. Paul St. Steven thought she was an airhead. He had insulted her, perhaps believing that noticing the insult was beyond her ability, as well.

"So you traveled thousands of miles to verify my inadequacies?"

Anger broke into his voice at last. "I traveled thousands of miles to attend a gathering of independent perfumers!"

"I'm a perfumer!"

Paul looked around him contemptuously. "Really?" He walked to the back of the oblong room. "Is this your scent organ?" He pointed to the multitiered rack holding small vials of oils and essences. "There must be—" he gestured expansively "—as many as fifty scents here." His voice was heavily sarcastic.

Stung, Hillary replied, "That's a small one for the festival. I didn't bring my main scent organ. This isn't my normal place of business."

"Ah, yes. I visited the famous little Scentsations."

Hillary's eyes narrowed. She was fiercely proud of her small but elegant store. Moving into Buffalo Bayou Mall had been one of her dreams. "Buffalo Bayou is a very prestigious location."

"Is it your only store—apart from this?" Again, he gestured and managed to suggest sarcasm with the movement.

"No," Hillary was relieved to be able to tell him. She began packing the rest of her bottles, filled with copies of well-known fragrances and a few of her own mixtures, into small padded boxes. "Three years ago, my partner and I split Scentsations into two different stores. She stayed at the original location and I moved into the mall. I target a crystal type of customer and she focuses on the natural, vegetarian, bake-bread-from-scratch type."

"And what is a crystal customer?" Paul began picking up bottles and reading the labels of the perfumes Hillary hadn't yet packed.

"Your customer."

Paul laughed, a deep mocking laugh devoid of amusement. "Stick to the bakers," he advised, setting the bottle down. "There are more of them and they're easier to please."

Hillary heard the bitterness in his voice and was immediately intrigued. He wasn't so much angry as disappointed, frustrated even. Why? Because of a missed seminar? "Do you speak from experience?"

"I speak from logic." He looked through the connecting door into her partner's crowded room as he spoke, giving Hillary a chance to study him.

He was very attractive, but very contained. His eyes spoke more than he did. Hillary wondered if he realized that.

If she were to create a scent for him, it would be a complex one, like the man. Not spicy, but smooth, heavy and musky.

"Your seminar was a good idea," he said, turning back to her. "What happened?"

Hillary hesitated.

"I think I'm entitled to an explanation."

"No, you're not."

Paul's jaw hardened as he clenched his teeth. "I have been put to a lot of inconvenience—"

"That's your fault. If Your Majesty had bothered to register instead of merely *informing* us—three days in advance—that you were going to attend, I could have told you the seminar never got off the ground!"

"And how could it have, with you in charge!"

"You don't know anything about me!"

"I know that you're a tiny businesswoman with big ideas!"

"Which is better than being a giant with no ideas!" Hillary's head, encased in a padded headpiece, began to pound.

"This—" Paul paused in frustration and waved his arms around "—is nothing! A table at a country fair!"

"Scentsations is my main business."

"Ah, yes. The crystal closet."

"Business is fine, thank you very much!"

"I didn't ask."

"You wouldn't. You'd decree."

Paul blinked and his lips parted slightly.

He looked magnificent in his anger, Hillary thought. He was in the throes of a full Gallic snit.

"I couldn't help overhearing." Melody, Hillary's partner, entered the room. "And neither could anyone else."

Hillary looked at the small crowd of interested customers in Melody's shop. "Rehearsals," she called with a forced smile. Sweeping them a deep curtsy she inclined her head. "Bow or something!" she hissed at Paul.

She could feel his anger. It radiated from him, just as hers pounded through her veins. Yet, she was strangely exhilarated by her encounter with him.

Hillary remained in her pool of velvet until she sensed Paul's rigid movement at her side. There was scattered applause and the people continued their browsing.

The interruption had brought Hillary to her senses. She'd been engaged in an undignified shouting match with a *representative from St. Etienne*. Had she lost her mind?

She raised her head and met his rueful brown eyes. He held out his hand, which she grasped, feeling the solid square warmth.

"My deepest apologies," he said as he helped her disentangle herself from her skirts.

Hillary brushed dust from the heavy velvet. "My deepest acceptance."

Melody stepped forward. "I'm Melody Anderson, Hillary's partner." She offered her hand to Paul.

He shook it, his impeccable social facade restored.

"We're so sorry for the misunderstanding," she said. "We did try to reach you."

"I was in Canada, visiting our Montreal boutique. My apologies for causing you any inconvenience," he said, and then looked surprised at his words.

Hillary smiled to herself. Calm, peaceful Melody had that effect on people. No one could get into a shouting match with Melody because she never shouted back.

"I would like to know what happened. Miss Simpson refused to tell me."

"I did not. I said you weren't *entitled* to know."

"The heat in here makes her grumpy." Melody urged them toward the door. "And you're exhausted from traveling all day. Have something to drink and enjoy the festival for a little while."

By the time Melody had finished speaking, Paul and Hillary found themselves outside the cottage.

"She reminds me of my nanny," Paul said, as he watched Melody serenely return to her customers.

Hillary lifted her head to catch the slight breeze. "It *is* cooler under the pines."

"Would you care for something to drink?"

"That sounds very civilized."

"I usually am."

Hillary chuckled. "Yes, I would like something to drink. A strawberry slush, I think."

A dusty haze hung in the air, stirred up by the tramping of thousands of feet. It outlined the beams of late-afternoon sun, adding to the otherworldliness of the festival. Following the smoky smell of cooking food, they wandered slowly past the jumble of cottages built to resemble a medieval European village until they came to the Queen's Tavern. As they bought slushes, served in wooden cups, trumpets sounded.

Hillary pushed a tight sleeve up her arm and exposed an anachronistic wristwatch. "Jousting, right on time."

Paul smiled down at her and Hillary momentarily forgot everything. It was probably one of his standard suave, continental, Frenchman looks, the kind he wore to entrance provincial American girls.

His lips curved with lazy sensuality as his eyes looked at her. Only at her. As if the thoughts behind them were only of her. "Shall we?" he asked quietly, still holding her gaze with his.

"What?" Hillary breathed.

Paul's smile deepened, showing even white teeth against tanned skin. "I haven't jousted in some time." His deep voice had the same tone he might have used to say, *I've been waiting for you all my life.*

Hillary inhaled deeply, feeling the edge of her costume's scooped neckline strain against her chest. He *knew.* He knew how he affected her. He probably affected a lot of women the same way. He represented a great designer-clothing house with its own perfumes; he'd know a lot about women.

Was there amusement lurking in those brown eyes? Hillary mentally doused herself with a bucket of cold water. "I suppose it's like riding a bicycle—you never forget how." She chose a bright cheerleader smile from her own repertoire and drew him into the crowd.

As they reached the racing track, the spectators roared. Chariots, knights in armor and horses draped in vivid fabric paraded past.

"Good against evil, I presume?" Paul gestured at the black knight and his opponent dressed in the king's colors. The king, queen and assorted courtiers presided in a box above the playing field. A young woman dropped a filmy handkerchief to the king's knight.

"She's the prize," Hillary said.

"Then we must favor the black knight. Evil is so much more interesting than good, don't you agree?"

"I don't know. That doesn't sound quite right."

"I didn't say preferable, I said more interesting."

The black knight won his match and vanquished two other foes. He taunted the crowd, demanding a champion and defender for the crown.

The princess swooned.

Hooves thundered and a knight in silver and pale blue rode out of the forest. A champion for the people. Loud cheering marked his entrance as the crowd enthusiastically participated in the medieval drama. Paul joined his voice with theirs, surprising Hillary.

"I thought you were rooting for evil."

"The newcomer is not entirely good. He waited until the black one was weakened by the others before making himself known."

"So you like your good laced with a bit of sneakiness." As the surging crowd jostled Hillary, Paul placed a steadying hand on her arm. "Did I say that?"

"You didn't have to."

Paul shrugged, giving Hillary an enigmatic smile. He held on to her arm until they were nearly back at the tall pine outside her cottage. Paul would be the kind of man who showed women such small courtesies. Hillary felt feminine, without feeling diminished.

When they reached the tree, Hillary sank onto the wooden bench surrounding the trunk and patted the place beside her. "About the seminar," she began as he sat beside her. "The only reason it didn't come off is that I don't have any clout. I didn't have a big name backing me—if I'd known you were interested, it would have helped. The hotels in the mall would only commit space on a contingency basis. If someone bigger or with a track record came along, then I'd have to pay a substantial deposit to hold the rooms. That's exactly what happened—someone else wanted to reserve this weekend and I just didn't have the money."

"I see." Paul sighed heavily.

"And I realize that I should have planned further in advance, but I still need a big name or big bucks."

"I see," he repeated, his expression bleak.

He seemed even more disappointed than she had been. Hillary found herself trying to comfort him. "I've been corresponding with everyone who requested more information. I'll have my seminar. The independents want one."

"I only just saw the spring issue of *Perfumer's Quarterly* when I was in Montreal."

"The retraction was in the summer issue." And wasn't very large, not nearly as large as the original notice. The tone implied that Hillary had canceled the seminar, not that the advertisement had appeared by mistake. Hillary wondered if any other seminar participants would be waiting for her back in Houston.

"That'll teach me to fall behind in my reading." Paul seemed to be trying for a light tone, but failed.

"Why did you drive all the way up here?" Hillary asked.

Paul shook his head. "Frustration, I suppose. The hotel knew nothing of your seminar, the mall people knew nothing, and your assistant said you were here." He shrugged. "So I came."

Hillary couldn't interpret his obvious disappointment. There was more to this than just a wasted trip. "As long as you've traveled all this way. I'd like to show you my...crystal closet."

Paul's eyes closed briefly. "Again, my apologies," he said, his deep voice vibrating with sincerity, his smile calculated to win her forgiveness. "It would give me great pleasure to tour your perfumery."

"You're forgiven." How could she refuse that smile? She was a woman, after all.

CHAPTER TWO

"WHAT'LL I WEAR?" Hillary jogged in place in front of her closet while an aerobics video played in the background. Sophisticated and polished, that was the look she wanted. Of course, that was the look she always wanted. To be...sultry. But brunettes were sultry. Frenchwomen were sultry. Hillary Simpson was not, and never would be, sultry.

It wasn't for lack of trying. Hillary broke her jogging rhythm and reached for a black gabardine suit. She wore a lot of black, hoping the color would elevate her blond bubbliness to an icy sophistication. She chose an emerald silk blouse that matched her eyes, tossed the clothes onto her bed and jogged back into the living room.

The exercise instructor, who managed to look sultry even though she was a blonde, was doing lunges. Hillary hated lunges and usually got her breakfast during this part of the video. Today, she turned off the tape since she was eating leftover chocolate-chip cookies from the Renaissance Festival. She couldn't face her video instructor after she'd skipped lunges *and* eaten chocolate-chip cookies. At least they were whole wheat.

Hillary felt slightly queasy as she walked in the back entrance of Scentsations. She told herself it was the cookies and not nerves caused by the coming meeting with Paul St. Steven. Usually she enjoyed walking right through the front of the shop and admiring the crystal and amber glitter of the perfumes.

"Hillary, did that man ever get hold of you?" Natasha, Hillary's assistant, popped a huge bubble, catching part of the gum on her nose. She giggled as Hillary sternly pointed at the trash can.

Hillary sighed faintly. Even Natasha looked sultry. She was eighteen, clad in a black knit minidress and tights. She weighed about two pounds, had black hair worn in an exotic geometric cut and generous lips stained scarlet. Hillary had hired her solely for her looks. She thought they contrasted nicely with her own.

"Did he?" Natasha repeated. "I told him you were at the festival and he asked for directions. You didn't tell me what to say if he asked for directions."

"I didn't think he would. In fact, I'm surprised he didn't receive one of the thousand or so messages I left for him."

"Well, I gave him directions." Natasha began to count the float.

"I know." Hillary nodded. "He found me. He's coming back here for a tour of the shop today."

"Shouldn't take long." Natasha bent to retrieve a fallen bill, making Hillary wince.

"Natasha, I'll do that. Would you restock the perfumes we brought back from the festival? They're in the lab." Hillary finished preparing the cash register for business, then unloaded the scent organ she had taken to the festival. She liked to display it near the front of the glass-walled shop.

"Good morning." The familiar deep voice sounded from just behind her. Paul stood on the other side of the security gate that ran across the storefront.

Hillary was annoyed to find that he looked even more attractive when he was rested. "Good morning," she replied, with a cheerful professionalism she'd practiced in the car on the drive to work. "Ready for the grand tour?" She unlocked the metal gate and pulled it open.

Paul tilted his head as white teeth tugged at his lower lip. "I would like nothing better, but in a few moments I must leave for an appointment. I'm meeting the manager of Pavilion—do you know it?"

Hillary crossed her arms in front of her. "This mall's closest competitor? Of course I know it."

His face brightened. "You shop there, then?"

It was designer row, the stratospheric prices far above a working girl's budget. Was he insulting her? She thought not. "Sometimes." Shop, yes. Buy, no.

"Pavilion might be a good place for a St. Etienne boutique."

So naturally, *their* appointment took second place.

"The manager was only available this morning, and I'm glad, because it gives me the opportunity to have dinner with you." Paul walked toward her as he spoke, watching her. When he stopped, he was just a shade closer than a stranger should stand.

Hillary took an involuntary step backward, immediately feeling gauche and naive. *Sultry, think sultry,* she told herself. "All right."

Paul's gaze lingered on her features a moment. He had a way of bending his head so that his eyes met hers, instead of looking down his nose the way many men—and women—did. It made her very aware of him. "I'll come back later this afternoon, then we'll leave for a barbarically early dinner."

"I'll look forward to it."

Paul smiled another dazzling smile. "Au revoir."

"Ciao," Hillary said brightly, and immediately wished she hadn't. The echoes of Paul's softly amused chuckle stayed with her for most of the day.

Was he playing a game with her? Was he mocking her? Or did he treat all women this way, upholding the Frenchman's code *d'amour?*

Code d'amour. What was the matter with her? Just because he was French didn't mean her virtue was in peril. Besides, she wanted to be a business associate, not a brief diversion.

Hillary flicked on the light in the back room that served as her office and small lab.

"Can I have my break now?" Natasha raised her eyebrows and gave Hillary a hopeful grin.

"Natasha, the store opens in five minutes," Hillary pointed out, carefully stretching her patience.

Natasha scooted toward her purse. "Yeah, but Toodle Lou's is having a sale today. My friend who works there is holding back this great little dress, but she's not supposed to—you know."

Hillary nodded. "I know."

"She'll get in trouble if she's caught. If I'm there when the store opens, it'll be okay."

Hillary waved her on. "Fifteen minutes. I want to work at the organ this morning. You think you can beat the crowd?"

"I *know* I can!" Natasha ran for the door. "My sister's fifth in line." Natasha had a twin. When she'd discovered Nanette, Hillary had hired her, too. Nanette lacked her sister's flamboyant style, but she made up for it in intelligence. Between them, Nanette and Natasha arranged their own work schedule. Everyone was happy.

Hillary smiled and went out front to the display organ, which she'd filled with some common scent combinations. Using those as a base, she saved time when creating a personalized fragrance. Right now, she was designing a signature fragrance for Toodle Lou's. Hillary hoped Lou would be flattered and agree to sell the perfume in her popular and trendy store.

The scent would have to be unusually exotic. Hillary started with tuberose oil. It was one of the most expensive at $2,000 a pound, but Toodle Lou's wasn't cheap. White Shoulders and Chloé used tuberose. And jasmine. All the *grands parfums* contained jasmine.

Hillary's ultimate goal was to link one of her perfumes with a fashion designer, preferably one who didn't already have a fragrance bearing his or her name. To remain financially solvent, most couturiers eventually marketed a perfume. Women who could not afford designer clothes could afford the perfumes.

Hillary had hoped to make contacts at her seminar. She needed just one successful perfume. Just one hit, and fame and fortune, especially fortune, would be hers.

There would also be enough money to split Scentsations and Earth Scents. She and Melody had been taking the two stores in different directions; dissolving their partnership would be a relief. She knew Melody felt the same way, but Melody would never mention it first. The problem was that they couldn't afford to dissolve their partnership until Scentsations was firmly established. Hillary could barely afford the rent increases, which occurred with depressing regularity. If Scentsations failed and she was forced to give up her hard-won space in one of the most exclusive malls in Houston, she wanted to be able to return to Earth Scents.

Money would solve that problem. Of course, money solved most problems. And a hit perfume meant money.

Perhaps there'd even be enough left over to shop at Pavilion.

Hillary shook her head slightly. Wait a minute. Fate had sent a representative from St. Etienne to Houston and she'd agreed to have dinner with him. She had fantasized about a chance like this. Fate would never forgive her if she bungled it.

Hillary was returning the vials of essence to the racks as Natasha loped back into the shop, triumphantly carrying her prize.

A bubbly Natasha was always good for business. It meant Hillary could work in the back all day, and the shop wouldn't suffer. And that was important, because when Paul St. Steven returned for his tour, Hillary intended to give him samples of her two best perfumes, Sun Shimmers and Moon Shadows, and a well-rehearsed sales pitch. It was a long shot, but she had to try.

By five o'clock, Hillary had poured generous samples of her perfumes into her best bottles. She had computed sales figures and packaging-design ideas. She had mapped out two advertising campaigns with cost breakdowns. She had written and was memorizing her speech. She was ready.

"He's here!" Natasha announced in a stage whisper Hillary knew Paul must have heard.

Hillary forgot her speech.

"He's not bad for an older guy," Natasha added as Hillary left her desk, deciding that a casual, spontaneous approach was best, after all.

Only Paul's profile was visible as he stared out the window watching the shoppers. Older? Just the barest hints of silver shone at his temples, but his face wore a weight-of-the-world look.

He masked it immediately when he saw her.

Maybe mid-thirties, Hillary decided. Not that much older than she in years, just in experience.

"This is a wonderful location," Paul said. "Your shop can be seen from three directions. Did you design the front?"

Hillary smiled. Compliments on Scentsations always made her happy. "Location in the mall was luck, but I extended the windows."

"Very smart. Traffic must go around it. People will notice the store."

"That's what I intended." Hillary caught herself grinning madly, responding to his praise like an eager puppy.

"Ta-ta," Natasha sang, timing her exit so that her foot crossed the threshold at exactly five-thirty. Hillary turned to wave and caught sight of Paul's reflection in the glass.

The mask had slipped again. His meeting must not have gone well.

"Can we expect a St. Etienne's outlet here in Houston?" she asked.

Paul shrugged. "Not for some time. Houstonians are young and vibrant."

And St. Etienne's clothes are not, Hillary supplied silently.

"We are more couture-oriented. For the woman of a certain age who desires beautiful, well-made clothes that will last." He smiled, as if in apology. "You Houston women must mature a little first."

And Hillary saw the Light. It truly was a blinding flash, knocking all other thoughts from her mind. St. Etienne needed a rejuvenation shot. St. Etienne was old-fashioned—fashionable, but old. They needed to tap into the younger market. And Hillary Simpson would point the way.

Paul was vulnerable right now. He felt guilty for canceling their appointment and she planned to take advantage of that, right after she figured out exactly what Paul's position with St. Etienne was. "Is this what you do for St. Etienne? Are you a salesman?"

Paul wore a peculiar expression. "I suppose I am. I do a little of everything."

"Except perfumery."

"Except perfumery." Paul added nothing else and Hillary didn't want to antagonize him unnecessarily by prying.

"I feel that way, too, sometimes," she said lightly, glossing over the potentially awkward moment. "You can see the scent bottles and perfume accessories we sell in addition to perfumes." She waved to indicate the glass cases and shelves.

"Who is your perfumer?" Paul asked.

"*I* am."

Paul looked surprised. "Your scent organ is obviously for display, so I naturally assumed that you used one of the large chemical firms, or that your main office supplied you with perfumes and mixtures."

"This is *my* shop. It's an independent."

"Once again, I must apologize." Paul headed toward the cluster of sample bottles. "Fabulous fakes. Fragrance shouldn't cost a fortune," he read. "How naughty of you," he said with an admonishing click of his tongue.

Hillary smiled unrepentantly. "Not at all. If I said those *were* the originals, that would be naughty."

"Rather more than naughty, I should think."

"Besides, imitation is the sincerest form of flattery."

"But doesn't pay any royalties." Paul picked up a small paper blotter and dipped it into a tester, then sniffed. "Not bad," he said of her copy of a currently popular perfume. "Though not everyone would be fooled."

"It's close enough." Hillary leaned against the glass counter, watching as he stared at the display. He had a nice, well-shaped profile. "I doubt that my sales will put much of a dent in St. Laurent's thirty-five or so million in royalties."

"I suppose I should be grateful you haven't attempted a copy of Volitaire or Sainte," he commented, naming two well-known St. Etienne perfumes introduced more than fifty years ago. He looked at her as he spoke, his lips curved in a smile that invited her to share his amusement.

She started to respond, then stopped.

His smile faded when he saw Hillary's stricken look. "Ah." He nodded slightly and sighed.

"I..."

"You haven't copied them because no one has asked." He had read the truth on Hillary's face.

"I know them, of course," she said, trying to recover. "They're classics. Heavy, sensuous, complex."

"Yes." Paul's voice was clipped. "Each has several hundred ingredients."

"You see, I couldn't begin to do them justice." Hillary clasped her hands together. She did this automatically when agitated because she tended to gesture with them more than she should. "If you advertised—"

"It's all right, Hillary," Paul said, using her name for the first time.

She liked the way he said it, with the syllables poured slowly like honey. He reached out and caressed her cheek lightly with his thumb, curling his fingers beneath her chin and urging it upward with the softest of touches.

In his eyes, she saw that he was aware of her attempt to spare him the small embarrassment. His expression held amusement and gratitude, before his hand dropped to her elbow. "And now I must see your laboratory," he said, motioning toward the back.

A subdued Hillary escorted Paul to the small back room.

"There would have been no question that a perfumer was in residence if I had see this earlier," Paul commented as he went directly to Hillary's scent organ.

The wooden structure curved in a semicircle atop a table and extended eight racks high. Each rack contained more than one hundred vials. "Quite an investment for you."

Hillary took a deep breath. "A gift from my parents. One I didn't deserve." She smiled to herself. "I think of them when I use it, and I'm determined not to let them down."

"Good. You are serious." As Paul spoke, Hillary thought she heard a new respect in his voice. She was pleased.

"How I wish..." His voice trailed off and he turned with a determined smile. "I made early reservations at my hotel's restaurant. It's here in the mall."

"The Brookfield?"

Paul nodded. "Yes. You did say the seminar was to be held there."

"I'd hoped." Hillary made a face. "I may still pull one off."

He gave her a long appraising look. "Perhaps you could."

Especially if she could announce his attendance. "I intend to."

Nanette's arrival left them free to walk down the glittering mall, which was already partially decorated for Christmas. "I had hoped to use your seminar to announce a contest awarding a study grant at St. Etienne to a promising young perfumer." Regret sounded in Paul's voice.

Hillary stopped, grabbing Paul's arm. "That's wonderful...would have been wonderful. This would be...if I had known ... if you had only told me..."

Paul covered her hand, which still gripped his arm. Embarrassed by her babbling, Hillary drew her hand away, but he captured it and tucked it into his elbow, walking her in a courtly promenade. "The idea only occurred to me when I saw your announcement in *Perfumer's Quarterly*. The seminar seemed the perfect opportunity to meet with perfumers."

"It *would* be the perfect opportunity. Did you plan to have just one perfumer studying at St. Etienne?"

Paul shrugged. "A grant for one, an invitation for others, perhaps?"

"Yes! Paul, if we work together on this..."

"Together?"

Hillary, filled with renewed hope, ignored his doubtful look and barreled on. "It will be the best independent perfumers' seminar ever held. St. Etienne is incredibly generous—"

"No, no." Paul shook his head emphatically. "You mustn't cast me in the role of philanthropist. *If* such a thing came to pass, St. Etienne would receive a lot of publicity. I don't know—we might, if it were good enough, you understand, release the perfume he—"

"Or *she*," Hillary interjected.

Paul inclined his head in acknowledgment. "Or she composes. But it is academic now." He *was* disappointed, she could tell.

"It doesn't have to be." So St. Etienne was receptive to a perfume from an outsider. As they entered the restaurant foyer, Hillary clenched her purse straps in excitement. Before they'd left the shop, she'd slipped the samples of her own perfumes inside. She would have to wait for just the right moment to present them.

"Your table will be ready in a few minutes," said the maître d'. "Would you care to wait in the bar?"

Hillary sighed impatiently. She hated it when restaurants did that. There was no excuse for making them wait this early on a Monday night. She looked pointedly at her watch, at the maître d' and then at the bar. A brunette in a gold-sequined dress was draped over one end, and a dark-haired businesswoman wearing a mustard-colored suit was reading the *Wall Street Journal* at the other. Hillary glanced into the dining room, watching as an attractive couple with Latin good looks was seated. Hillary noticed the man's well-cut brown suit and his companion's gilded silk evening gown.

"Hillary?"

She glanced up at Paul, trying to stem the beginning of a flush. He'd seen her fidgeting and must think she was an impatient child.

Paul studied her for a moment, then leaned forward and murmured to the maître d'. Without a word, the man beckoned them to follow him.

She absorbed the warmth of Paul's hand on her back as he guided her to the table. He was being very courteous, very civilized. Hillary liked him better when he was laughing at her or angry with her, anything but this cool politeness.

He seemed preoccupied tonight. Hillary was sure his well-mannered smile held a tinge of disappointment. Why? What *had* happened this afternoon? Did his job depend on his getting the rights to open a St. Etienne boutique? Would he be reprimanded for wasting the company's money by coming to Houston to attend her seminar? Hillary felt a prickle of guilt, even though she knew she wasn't at fault.

When they reached their table, Paul had to wait a moment as a couple was seated at the table behind them. The woman caught Hillary's attention. Here was a clear-cut example of dressing to please a man. Gold lamé plunged deeply front and back; a full skirt fluttered in the air-conditioning. The woman tossed a mane of jet-black hair over her shoulder and gazed into her escort's eyes.

Hillary's gaze returned to *her* escort's eyes, noting the fine lines in the corners. They had seen much, those eyes.

She managed to confine herself to social small talk until the waiter brought their salads. Then she couldn't stand it any longer. No matter that the odor of the vinaigrette dressing would interfere with her perfumes. Charming though he remained, Paul was very obviously frustrated about the St. Etienne boutique and the failure of her seminar to materialize. Hillary thought she could help.

"It's too bad St. Etienne won't have a boutique here. But your fashions have a reputation for being rather...exclusive." She'd been about to say "staid and pricey." "Perhaps if you target a younger market."

Paul's look became stern. "We have our own designer..."

"And a good one, I'm sure," Hillary agreed quickly. "But who's your public relations firm? Why don't you have any commercials and promotions?"

Paul made a sound somewhere between a surprised laugh and a cough. "My dear Hillary, St. Etienne doesn't need to advertise, other than the occasional print ad in *Vogue* or one of the other fashion bibles."

Not advertise? Hillary felt like screaming. "Oh, I never meant to suggest that you *need* to advertise. As you said, the clothes are for women of a certain age.... Well, you see, I've got this idea." Hillary leaned forward. "You have clothes and you have perfumes."

Paul nodded perfunctorily, his eyes flicking past Hillary's shoulder.

"Look at Chanel. Look what they've done. They're popular again."

"I was unaware that Chanel had ever retired from being fashionable." Paul dabbed his mouth with a napkin. "Do you wear Chanel?" he asked in a transparent attempt to steer the conversation away from St. Etienne.

"Occasionally," Hillary replied abruptly, deciding that the Chanel lipstick in her purse counted. "But back to St. Etienne—most women can't afford your clothes."

"Hillary—"

"It's okay. I have a proposal to fix all that."

Paul put his fork down and settled back in his chair. "Somehow, I thought you would."

"Yes," Hillary continued, undeterred by the resignation she saw in his face. "St. Etienne could be the first fashion house where a perfume launched a line of clothes. Introduce a new young scent. Women will become accustomed to the St. Etienne name and then want clothes to go with the image. You'll have your younger customers *and* your Pavilion boutique."

Paul's face was a dull red. She'd ignored his gentle warnings and gone too far. Maybe Paul wasn't the person she should approach, she realized belatedly, her enthusiasm tempered.

"Perfumes take years to develop." The words were clipped, his salad abandoned.

Her cue. Hillary reached into her purse. "I have two perfumes. Sun Shimmers and Moon Shadows."

"We have a perfumer," Paul said at once.

Hillary knew he was angry with her, but it was too late to stop. She had to get all the way through her proposal because this was the only chance she'd have. "He hasn't released a new perfume in years!"

The ruddiness vanished abruptly as Paul's jaw tightened. Aware that she'd hit a sore spot but not knowing why, Hillary continued speaking. "And these don't require extensive aging. Just about as long as it would take to put together an advertising campaign. Think of the time you'd save. These are modern perfumes for modern women. Women who exercise and play tennis. These aren't coddled women. They sweat."

Paul was smiling again and Hillary cringed inwardly at his patronizing amusement. "Alluring as the thought of sweating women is, I must decline—"

"Can you decline?" Just because she wasn't with a big-time company didn't mean her ideas should be dismissed out of hand. "What I mean is, should I speak with someone else in St. Etienne management?"

An incredulous expression crept across Paul's features. Anger mixed with something else. Hadn't anyone ever challenged him? Paul wore an air of authority as if entitled to, not because he had a puffed-up sense of his own importance. Maybe he was a big deal at St. Etienne.

In that case, her failed seminar had cost more than she'd imagined.

He struggled visibly for control. Intrigued, Hillary wondered what would happen if he lost it. Would he create a magnificent scene?

"You're quite outrageous you know," he said with a strangled laugh. "I do believe you are the only person who would dare say such things to me."

"Maybe someone should!" Before she'd even finished speaking, Hillary wanted to bite her tongue. She had gone way, way too far.

Paul crumpled his napkin and dropped it beside his plate, clearly preparing to leave.

"Please—"

"You are my dinner guest. We should leave before I forget."

Much to Hillary's relief, their waiter appeared, carrying a bottle of French champagne, its gold foil top gleaming above a chocolate-brown velvet bow. "Compliments from the brunette in gold."

Paul sat as if turned to stone, staring fixedly at the cream envelope attached to the champagne.

"Aren't you going to open it?" Hillary asked, hoping the diversion would make him forget her ill-advised words. "The card *or* the champagne," she said, when Paul didn't move. "Hmm." She crinkled her nose. "Whoever your friend is, she wears a marvelous fragrance." Hillary inhaled deeply. "I don't know it," she said, amazed, breaking off as she finally noticed Paul's twisted smile.

He slowly lifted the flap of the small envelope. The sweet smell intensified. Paul closed his eyes briefly and fumbled slightly with the card.

Who was this brunette in gold? *A past lover.* Hillary was intrigued that the thought bothered her. Curiously, she looked at nearby tables, searching for the mysterious woman, then the significance of their fellow diners dawned on her.

"I don't believe this!" Her whispered words brought a questioning look from Paul.

"They're all—" Over his shoulder, Hillary saw Ms. Gold Lamé, Madame Gilded Silk, and a matronly gold brocade. "Every woman within sight is a brunette wearing gold."

Someone had gone to a great deal of trouble for this display of...what? Hillary picked up the cream-colored card, curiosity overcoming politeness. "Dominique." The word was scrawled in chocolate-brown ink. "Well, Dominique, whoever you are, you've certainly got style."

"I..."

"It's okay." Hillary reached across the table and patted Paul's hand reassuringly. She could be sophisticated about this. After all, *she* was with Paul and Dominique was not.

On the other hand, she didn't intend to hang around and have Paul distracted by any more of Dominique's elaborate stratagems. She tried to catch their waiter's attention, difficult since he seemed to be staring anywhere but at them. He *should* be embarrassed.

Her anger began to simmer. Wasn't the man at least planning to open the champagne for them? Hillary stood abruptly. Embarrassed or not, the waiter wasn't about to let them leave without paying the check. She extracted her business card from her purse, beckoned to Paul and, as an afterthought, grabbed the bottle. Champagne was champagne, after all.

Giving Paul a blinding smile, she draped her free hand over his arm. "Let's blow this joint."

Paul was startled into a laugh. Hillary determinedly strode toward the maître d', the waiter hurrying after them making little noises of protest.

When they got to the bar, Paul reached in front of Ms. Mustard Suit, took two champagne glasses and winked at Hillary. She winked back. Dominique was going to have some competition.

Hillary slapped her card on the maître d's reservation book. "Send the bill to Dominique—with my compliments."

CHAPTER THREE

"ISN'T THIS BETTER?" Hillary and Paul were seated side by side in the food court atrium overlooking the mall.

"Much." Only the jerky movement of his fingers betrayed his inner agitation. "You are an amazing woman."

Hillary started to peel the gold foil from the champagne, then changed her mind and handed the bottle to Paul. He had already shredded his cocktail napkin.

She took a handful of the salted bar snacks she'd grabbed to go with the champagne and regarded him thoughtfully. "You're new at this, aren't you?"

A smile stole about his lips and widened. He chuckled softly. There were slight dimples to go with the cleft in his chin. Even white teeth flashed briefly, but the amused look remained on his face. "I've opened a few champagne bottles in my time."

Now Hillary laughed. "I meant being pursued by a woman. I'm not going to pry, but obviously you and Dominique..."

"*You* not pry?" Paul threw back his head and laughed uninhibitedly, drawing glances from some of the shoppers. "Hillary, you're delightful." He poured her some champagne, then leaned forward on one elbow, chin resting in his hand, and gave her a long look. "When a woman and I part, we remain friends. A relationship should never continue after ceasing to bring pleasure."

Hillary cleared her throat. "Sounds very continental. You must have a lot of friends."

"More friends than enemies."

Hillary tasted her champagne, suddenly feeling that she was out of her league.

"But you are right, I have been pursued. Dominique would like to merge."

"I'll just bet she would," Hillary muttered into her champagne glass.

Paul's teeth tugged at his lower lip. "Dominique Parfums."

"Oh." Her eyes widened as the information registered. They were the French fashion and perfume house that was making such a splash on this side of the Atlantic. *"Oh!"*

"My travel plans are not public knowledge and the thought of being followed here is disconcerting. The woman is quite persistent." There was a grim set to his mouth as he raised his champagne glass.

So there is a woman, Hillary thought. "What does she do for Dominique—other than buy you champagne on her company's expense account?"

This drew a small smile. "She's a vice president—an ambitious vice president."

Hillary bit her lip. "Sort of your counterpart here in the States?"

Paul shrugged a shoulder and sipped his champagne. "I suppose so."

Hillary mentally promoted Paul from salesman to vice president. She was impressed with herself. St. Etienne had sent a vice president to her seminar! Hillary Simpson was on her way! "Has she pulled any other stunts?"

Paul shook his head. "Nothing this elaborate. Mostly little messages, such as drawings combining the St.

Etienne white-rose logo with the Dominique brown bow
and a list of department stores that sell their clothes.
Once, a reinterpreted St. Etienne dinner gown was delivered to my hotel. Always something to let me know
she is aware of where I am, no matter how discreet I
think I've been. Which is why you had trouble finding
me. My people tend to be overprotective."

After hearing all that, Hillary wondered how Ms.
Dominique *had* managed to find Paul. "Why does she
continue when it bothers you?"

"She—" he paused "—is trying to demonstrate her
creativity, as well as the financial resources of Dominique Parfums. She obviously hired actors and turned
the entire restaurant into a gold-and-brown Dominique
commercial. An extravagant gesture conceived and ex-
ecuted in a matter of hours."

*But not very smart if it alienates someone you want to
impress,* Hillary thought. "What fragrance is this?" She
reached for the card and sniffed. "Tuberose, ylang-ylang
and probably jasmine—great perfumes always have jasmine. I wonder what the top note is."

"Very good," Paul said, inclining his head. "Do you
think you could copy the scent?" he asked, after Hillary tossed the card back on the table.

"You mean you want a fabulous fake?" Hillary
grinned.

Paul studied her as he tilted the champagne flute to his
mouth, sipped, then set the glass on the table. "Maybe
I want to see how good you really are."

They were talking about perfumes, weren't they? Hillary swallowed. "Here, then." She reached into her
purse and set the vials of Sun Shimmers and Moon
Shadows on the table, flicking the scent-laden cream
card to one side.

She had annoyed him, she could see. Nevertheless, he reached for Sun Shimmers and opened the vial.

"Light, fresh, clean, woodsy, almost like a man's cologne," he pronounced as he replaced the stopper. "Your version of liberated womanhood?"

Hillary took a deep breath. Next to Dominique's perfume, hers smelled like a lightweight. "You haven't sampled any on skin. Here." She offered him her arm. "I wear Sun Shimmers. The perfume reacts with a woman's skin. The sun won't sour it or cause stains, and the scent isn't too heavy for hot weather."

Paul held her wrist and lowered his head. Hillary felt his breath against her arm before he inhaled. "Ah." His expression was startled. "Experimenting with pheromones? You amplify the woman's natural scent and it becomes part of the fragrance. This will be different on every woman. Much more than other perfumes." He still held her arm. "Do you wear scent on all the traditional pulse points?"

Hillary smiled. "And a few untraditional ones."

"Behind your ear?" Paul tugged her closer. "The other perfume interferes."

Nonplussed, Hillary leaned forward, angling her head. This time, Paul's breath against her neck sent a tingle down her back and raised goose bumps on her arms. She had a brief sense of the warmth of his skin and the cool softness of his hair before he slowly drew back, his eyes on hers. "Lovely."

"Thank you," she whispered.

In the short silence, Hillary felt her heart pound. He hadn't *done* anything, yet she felt as if her insides were about to be jolted loose.

"This fragrance isn't for every woman and would take unique marketing." He reached for Moon Shadows, but

Hillary's hand was there first. Her reaction to Paul's nearness concerned her. What would happen when he drew her close again?

"Uh, I think we're on sensory overload as it is. Moon Shadows is similar to the other—only for...night." Hillary couldn't meet his eyes. Paul St. Steven was not good for her composure. Feeling as she did, this was *not* the time to discuss exactly when Moon Shadows was at its most effective.

Hillary carefully boxed her samples and slipped them into her purse. When she did look up, she could see the knowing glimmer in Paul's expression. She picked up Dominique's card. "Let me try to copy this perfume."

"If you like."

"I thought you wanted me to."

"I'm curious to see what you can do." He hesitated. "I...have more of those cards. They're in my room."

"That would help. Let's go get them." Hillary had already stood up before she realized that she'd just invited herself to Paul's hotel room. Maybe she could bluff her way through this. "I hope you wrapped them in plastic," she said in the elevator.

"Of course."

She should have offered to wait in the lobby. Why hadn't she? He'd think she was a forward American woman with no class. She began to detest the extravagant sophistication of Dominique. And the scent that had been so alluring earlier, she now found cloying. It permeated the elevator.

When the doors opened, she expected the fragrance to dissipate. It didn't. If anything, the scent intensified. "I thought you said you wrapped those cards in plastic."

"I did," Paul said with a puzzled look at her.

The smell strengthened. Paul's steps slowed until he stood outside the door to his suite.

"It's coming from in there," Hillary said.

As Paul unlocked the door, an overpowering stench assailed them. Hillary's stomach lurched sickeningly as she followed Paul into the elegant living room.

"Roses!" Huge bouquets crowded every surface. "Dozens of white roses. I've never seen anything like this outside the movies. And then it's usually the woman's room."

"The white rose is the symbol of St. Etienne." Paul's voice was strained.

"You must like your work."

Paul gave her a reproachful glance. Then he asked, "Do you see a card?"

Hillary tweaked a familiar brown velvet bow, wrapped around gold tissue. Each bouquet was decorated the same way. "Do you really need one?"

"No." But he combed through the roses, anyway.

"Dominique's bow works well with the St. Etienne rose."

"How can you say that?" he asked, incensed. "The bow chokes the roses—the way Dominique would choke St. Etienne."

And the way he'd probably like to choke a nameless vice president right now, Hillary thought before peering into the bedroom. "Paul." She stood at the door and pointed.

Paul strode to the doorway. On his pillow rested a rose-shaped card made of heavy cream stock. Attached by a gold cord was a small vial filled with amber-colored liquid. The brown-inked message read, "We belong together—Dominique."

Hillary was having a difficult time separating Dominique the company from its unbelievable vice president.

"This is unconscionable. Is no one in this hotel able to refuse a bribe?" Paul turned to her in anger.

"Apparently not." Hillary was also appalled. "You can't stay here. You couldn't breathe. That woman has more money than sense." Hillary walked into the living room. "There's another hotel in the mall. Would you like me to call them?"

"Yes, please. Then I can pack before my clothes are ruined."

Hillary had to escape the smell. The odor gave her a headache. She knew there was more to this perfume bombing than Paul had told her.

Moments later, he joined her by the elevator, luggage in hand.

"I spoke to the manager," Hillary told him, "and he'll send your bags to the other hotel."

Paul nodded his assent. "Let's leave."

He walked Hillary back to her shop. "You've been remarkably sanguine about everything."

"It's a ploy to get you to tell me what's really going on."

"Ah..." Paul sighed. "The Dominique people are reminding me of their offer, which I don't like."

The merger offer was to *Paul?* Then he must be at least an executive vice president! "What was wrong with it?"

Paul managed to smile. "The fact that the offer was made by Dominique."

"And the perfume? What's that all about?"

At her question, Paul's expression became closed, and Hillary knew he didn't want to discuss it. "Bait," he replied lightly.

"Isn't damaging hotel property a little extreme?"

"Now that was a miscalculation. A rare mistake, as was the liquid sample. It's the first I've been given."

Hillary felt sick. Her two perfumes were unique, but Dominique's perfume was a classic traditional. Exactly like something St. Etienne would have developed. "I could have the sample analyzed by gas chromatography for you," she offered reluctantly. "Then you would know the ingredients, but unfortunately, not the exact amounts used. The University of Houston has the machine."

They were outside her store. "It does?" Paul was incredulous. "But that's wonderful! I'll take the perfume there myself. I'm in a hurry to see the results." He grasped her shoulders and kissed her on both cheeks. "Thank you, Hillary. Until tomorrow."

"Sure." She managed a wan smile. Nothing like shooting herself in the foot.

"YOU TRIED TO SELL HIM your perfumes?" Melody stared at her in amazement.

Hillary took a deep breath, a hint of defensiveness creeping into her voice. "Why not? They're good."

"Yes, but . . ." Melody stopped arranging new jars of her moisturizing lotion on the shelves at Earth Scents, apparently trying to find words to express herself without insulting Hillary. "Not quite in the St. Etienne style, I think."

Like Dominique's perfume. "St. E doesn't need another heavy, complex perfume," Hillary stated, reassuring herself more than anything else. "I just have to convince Paul of that."

Melody and Hillary each worked one day a week at the other's store; today it was Hillary's turn at Earth

Scents. Since Melody was wasting valuable time just staring at her, Hillary began to stock the shelves.

"So how goes the campaign?" Melody asked.

Hillary sighed. "So far, he's been underwhelmed."

"Don't worry about it," Melody said slowly. "St. Etienne is a dinosaur."

Hillary already knew that. "St. E has an old, established reputation."

"That they've been riding for the last twenty or thirty years," Melody pointed out.

"Then Sun Shimmers is exactly what they need!" Hillary began with enthusiasm. "There's a huge potential market. It doesn't change or fade with the heat and sun. Just think, you can wear a perfume while you play tennis and sweat up a storm and the fragrance won't be affected by the sun, the heat, or the salt on your skin."

"Does it repel mosquitoes?"

Hillary ignored the sarcasm. "No, but it won't attract them. Sun Shimmers works with natural body scents, not against them. You're always advocating a return to nature, so you ought to appreciate that." She tapped the shelves. "Shouldn't you be writing down how many bottles of moisturizer you've stocked?"

"I don't bother."

Hillary knew Melody didn't bother, but she never gave up trying to convince her to keep better records. "Then how do you know how many you've sold and how quickly?"

Melody took the empty box from Hillary. "There's one full shelf. If I have to dust the lotions more than twice, then they aren't selling fast enough."

Hillary rolled her eyes. "How do you figure your profits?"

Melody handed her a box of soaps. "If we pay the bills and have money left over, then we've made a profit. Put those in the baskets, will you? Now, what did he say about your perfumes?"

Hillary wore a dreamy smile as she remembered the tingle Paul's closeness had caused. "He said they were unique."

"Hmm." Melody raised an eyebrow.

"Look, there isn't any of the green soap here." Hillary was trying to distract Melody.

"Celery," Melody said, identifying it. "I've had to refill the other baskets twice and that one not at all, so I knew it wasn't selling." Her expression was innocent.

"All right," Hillary grudgingly admitted defeat this time. "You know your stock, but what happens when you expand? You'll never keep track of what's selling in all your stores with this kind of casual record-keeping."

"But I don't want to expand. Quit changing the subject and tell me more about that gorgeous man."

Hillary prepared to argue, but abruptly changed her mind. "He wanted to announce a perfumer's grant at our seminar. I could just kick myself."

"So what was his excuse for dinner?"

"An apology for canceling our appointment." Hillary avoided Melody's eyes.

"Mmm."

"Quit matchmaking, Melody, I'm not his type. I'm not sleek and sultry. If I wore diamonds, everyone would assume they were fake. I look . . . peasanty."

Melody laughed. "Then maybe it's opposites attracting." She gestured to the vintage Volkswagen pulling up outside the store. "Customers."

"Wait'll you hear what happened at dinner." Hillary walked to the back of the shop allowing Melody to deal with the customers, in silent acknowledgment of the growing differences between the partners—and their clientele.

Hillary tried to accept the more casual atmosphere of Earth Scents. It was the site of the original Scentsations and in an older section of Houston. Although it was on the fringes of the restored museum area, the neighborhood had changed. Now college students rented many of the smaller bungalows. The liberal coffeehouse atmosphere suited Melody and her husband, Ben. They were innocent, gently aging flower children. Their ideas and values were admirable, but Hillary didn't feel they were practical in the harsh realities of business competition in a large city.

Hillary sat at the small table nestled in the only corner left for her products. There was very little demand for custom-blended perfumes at this location, so she stocked mostly one-note floral fragrances here.

Since she had opened the Buffalo Bayou store, most of her perfumes were displayed there, while Melody's homey concoctions remained here. Scentsations had changed just as the partners had changed. They'd long ago dropped the pretense of Scentsations I and II. This was just Earth Scents.

Earthy. That described Melody. Hillary covertly watched her wait on the two jeans-clad college students. Melody wore an embroidered Mexican peasant dress and sandals. Her long rippled hair was parted in the middle and she occasionally tucked it behind her ear. She wore no makeup, except her own moisturizing lotion.

Hillary glanced down at her silk dress. She had left the coordinating jacket in the closet. Even though the dress was simple, she felt out of place here.

"Hillary, are you real busy?"

Ben came in from the storeroom to stand by her desk, but she was so lost in thought, she barely heard him.

"Not really." She couldn't do any work on copying Paul's perfume here. She'd have to return to the lab in her own store.

Her own store. As Hillary followed Ben to the storeroom, she acknowledged that she'd come to think of Earth Scents as Melody's and Scentsations as hers.

"I've got the new shipment of oils and essences. Knowing what a stickler you are for counting and such, I thought you'd like to check the packing list."

Hillary sent him an exasperated look. "You'd probably just reach in and start using the stuff. What if you were shortchanged?"

"That doesn't happen so very often."

"Or you were sent Moroccan rose oil and charged for Bulgarian attar?"

Ben shrugged. "You'd probably be the only one who could smell the difference."

"One's half the price of the other for a reason, Ben."

With an exaggerated sigh, he took the computer printout from her, then pried open a box. "Hey, I'm working on something for your fancy-schmancy shop. They sold real well at the Renaissance Festival."

"Anything to avoid inventory, right?" Hillary grinned and grabbed the printout, tossing it on a nearby chair. "Show me."

Ben poured several small silver filigree balls into Hillary's palm. The wires formed a cage.

"Pomanders?" Hillary touched the delicate spheres.

"Very good." Ben shoved his hands into his worn jeans pockets. "Melody is making frankincense and myrrh gums to put in them. Body heat of the wearer releases the scent. After I've had more experience, I'll use gold."

"We'll have to put them on black cords to keep the cost down." Hillary had already begun to think about displays. "This is great! How many can you make in time for Christmas?"

Ben held out his hand for the balls. "More than if I have to waste time with busy work. Besides, we sold out last weekend, so I took the names and addresses of people who wanted to order."

"You win. I'll do the inventory." Hillary picked up another box and tore off the packing tape. "Taking orders was a good idea, but remember to ask for a check *before* you mail the merchandise."

"Sure." Ben studied the little balls. "Melody and the kids really like it up at the festival site. Away from the big city. You know, if there were any way we could afford to live—"

"I figured you'd be in here." Melody interrupted her husband. "Hillary, bring that box out front so I can hear about your dinner and watch the store. It's almost time for you to leave."

Abandoning a wistful-looking Ben, Hillary carried the box out of the storeroom and told Melody about Dominique Parfums.

Melody gently touched her on the arm. "There'll be other chances, Hillary. You'll hook up with a young, sporty designer and make your fortune."

Hillary shook her head impatiently. "I'm not giving up! All I have to do is persuade Paul to buy one of my perfumes." Hillary looked at Melody, daring her to disagree. "He's the best chance I've had so far."

"You won't be a failure if he doesn't buy your perfumes."

Hillary stood up and retrieved her jacket from the
closet. "But I'll be a success if he does."

CHAPTER FOUR

How could she convince him to buy her perfumes? Hillary eased her car into the midday traffic on the Southwest freeway. Dominique's—Hillary thought of the woman vice president as Dominique—restaurant stunt was flashy. Hillary wished it had occurred to her first. Dominique had flair, money and a head start. Not to mention a heavy-duty perfume.

All was not lost. Hillary had—for the moment—Paul, and was not without a few ideas of her own. Paul was set in his thinking because St. Etienne no longer monitored the pulse of the fashion industry. He underestimated the youth market. He needed to see their buying power in action.

Hillary swung into her parking place at the mall, turned off the ignition and sat, both hands gripping the steering wheel. Paul still owed her three-fourths of a dinner. It wasn't much to work with.

Moon Shadows. The name of her night perfume triggered an idea. Paul had never sampled it. Maybe tonight was the night.

Hillary could demonstrate the youth market, the appeal of her perfume and the fact that Dominique wasn't the only one with an idea or two up her sleeve. Feeling encouraged, Hillary got out of her car and headed toward Toodle Lou's, Natasha's favorite shop.

Lou proved to be cooperative—for a price. But it was a price Hillary was quite willing to pay. In exchange for the use of her store tonight, Lou wanted an exclusive Toodle Lou perfume to sell with her clothes. Since this was what Hillary wanted, too, she was doubly excited, but Lou wanted the perfume right away, and that had Hillary frowning as she walked through the door to her own shop. Even with the head start she had on Lou's perfume, she still had to work on Paul's. And Paul's copy of the Dominique perfume would take more time.

"Why the sad face?" a bouncy Natasha asked. "Have a fight with your boyfriend?"

"No," Hillary answered, rather than deny that Paul was her boyfriend. "I'll be at the organ in the back. Call me if you get too busy."

She decided to work on the copy first. *I want to see how good your really are,* Paul had said. With a gas chromatograph reading, she'd know roughly the amounts and ingredients of Dominique's perfume, but Paul would be impressed if she could fake it before she saw the printout.

Hillary sat at her organ and opened the plastic wrapping containing the scented notes Dominique had left Paul. Inhaling the sensuous fragrance, Hillary wondered why Dominique's vice president was going to such lengths to attract Paul.

We belong together—Dominique. With sudden insight, Hillary knew that the woman wasn't interested in just the company.

Let Ms. Dominique have Paul, Hillary decided, annoyed at the pang she felt. She wanted St. E's backing for her perfume, and Paul didn't appear to be the type of man who mixed business and pleasure.

So be it. Hillary would keep their relationship strictly business. She would no longer tingle at the sound of his deep voice. Her heart would no longer race after a brief touch. And when he looked at her with those worldly brown eyes, her imagination would no longer zoom out of control.

Resolutely, Hillary picked up the scented cards. Copying this perfume might be Paul's way of auditioning her. Fine. She'd show him what kind of perfumer she was. And if he couldn't use Sun Shimmers or its companion, Moon Shadows, then she'd ask for the opportunity to develop something else.

Hillary could only copy the middle and base notes of the perfume. Without a liquid sample, she couldn't be certain of the top note—the rapidly evaporating first impression of a perfume.

Hours passed as she worked at her organ. Using countless paper blotters, Hillary blended, sniffed, blended more, then started over, as she tried various scent combinations. The perfume was a heavy, rich Oriental type. Complex and sensuous, and above all, a perfume to make its wearer noticed.

"Hello, Hillary."

At the sound of the deep, familiar male voice, Hillary felt a giant prickle begin at the nape of her neck and shoot down her spine. Her pulse quickened. Her imagination ran riot.

She took a deep breath. "Paul," she said, in a purely professional welcome.

He approached her worktable. "Already making good progress? You are impatient." He reached over her, picked up a tiny vial and inhaled. "On the right track. This should help." He handed her the original sample and a lengthy computer printout with squiggly lines forming peaks and valleys.

Hillary barely glanced at the printout, instead turning her attention to the liquid sample Dominique had obligingly left. "No real surprises in the main ingredients," she said, after several brief sniffs. "Jasmine and roses. I knew it." She really wanted to find out what the top note was. It smelled like a variation on the eau-de-cologne fragrance.

"Let me try something." She plucked a vial from a rack in her organ and blended the contents with one of the three combinations she'd already mixed.

Paul wore an amused expression as he pulled up a chair next to her table.

Hillary tried to ignore him.

"What is that?"

"Good old-fashioned eau de cologne. Grape spirit, oil of neroli, bergamot, rosemary and lavender. Madame Du Barry used a ton of it."

Paul cupped his chin in his hand. "I know."

Hillary spared him a quick look. "St. E sell it to her?"

"We're not quite that old."

It was the perfect opening. "Some people think you are," she commented, with a sideways glance to see his reaction.

Paul's expression was faintly amused, almost indulgent. She knew it wasn't the kind of expression business people used with each other. But wait until dinner. *Then* he'd see she could be just as ambitious as Ms. Dominique.

"So," Hillary continued, still sniffing and mixing, "you know what's in the perfume. If I can copy it, so can your perfumer. But it's still a copy. St. E shouldn't copy. St. E should lead."

"The House of St. Etienne does lead," Paul said emphatically.

"*Did* lead," Hillary returned.

Paul stood and began to pace, then turned to face her again. "You . . . aren't a restful sort of a person, Hillary."

"Restful people never get anywhere." She pushed away from her worktable. "I want St. E to bring out my perfumes. You won't consider them because St. E hasn't sold any fragrances like mine before. I'm trying to convince you that they're exactly what St. E needs! Instead, you just want to copy somebody else's idea."

Hillary almost held her breath, thinking that she would really anger Paul.

"I have my reasons." He raised an eyebrow. "I don't suppose it would make any difference if I told you I didn't want to discuss them with you?"

"No."

"I thought not," Paul said as he returned to his chair beside Hillary's desk. He didn't look angry, which Hillary took as a good sign.

"You owe me part of a dinner," she said, with a determined smile.

"*That* I will discuss with you." Paul grinned broadly.

"Good." Hillary kept her voice briskly professional, though Paul and his grin evoked unprofessional flutters. "*I* made reservations this time."

Leaving Natasha in charge of Scentsations, Hillary drew Paul out into the glittering mall. She wandered slowly and deliberately past the flashy boutiques. "It's a week night, not quite the Christmas season, yet the stores are full, aren't they?"

"So it would appear."

They turned a corner. "*Most* of the stores are full." Hillary paused eloquently outside the store of a major designer—one that was a direct competitor of St. Etienne. Two saleswomen lounged indolently on the richly upholstered chairs in the waiting area.

"I know what you're up to, little gamine. However, one sale here—" Paul gestured with a nod of his head "—equals several anywhere else."

Hillary felt an entirely inappropriate pleasure at being called a "little gamine." She was well aware that it wasn't exactly a sign of respect in any language. Taking his arm, she steered him past a few more stores and turned another corner. "There." She pointed to Toodle Lou's. "Let's check out a few prices."

A line had formed outside the polished brass doors. "It's closed?" Paul asked.

"Only temporarily." She slanted a glance toward him, noting that he seemed only mildly curious. Just wait. "They're having a special promotion tonight." Hillary walked to the front of the line and knocked. After a saleswoman opened the door, they slipped inside, accompanied by murmurs of protest from those waiting in line.

Now that she was actually committed to her scheme, she felt nervous. "Why don't you look around while I change into something more comfortable?" Hillary had been silently practicing the movie line for the past several minutes. She returned wearing a floaty Zandra Rhodes creation.

"Lovely," a bemused Paul complimented her, as a scurrying salesclerk jostled him.

Hillary inhaled deeply. Moon Shadows had been spritzed liberally about. Paul's smile told her he had noticed. "The perfume, too."

"Except that you have to smell it on a woman before you experience the true scent."

The words had scarcely left her lips before Paul drew her close. For an instant, she felt surprise, but that was chased away by the nearness of his body. Dipping his head, Paul's eyes were on hers until the last possible moment. His face skimmed by her mouth, then moved to the side of her neck where she heard him inhale. His lips barely brushed her skin before he raised his head. "Perhaps I could sample it on some of the untraditional pulse points you mentioned—later."

Every one of those pulse points began to throb.

"Ready?" the saleswoman asked a weak-kneed Hillary.

Dazed, she nodded and the women whisked back a curtain, revealing the store's front display window, decorated with palm trees, sand, a midnight-blue backdrop, large yellow moon and a table set for two.

"Oh, no," Paul said, shaking his head and laughing.

Hillary, conscious of the interested people lined up outside the shop, gathered her filmy skirts and stepped into the window. "Oh, yes. And please note the sign."

Paul followed her to the table, twisting to read the sign in the window. "Moon Shadows, a Scentsational fantasy—anytime."

He turned to give Hillary a long inscrutable look before holding out a chair for her.

He had decided to humor her, Hillary saw. She sat down, breathing a small sigh of relief. "Did you have a chance to look at some of the clothes Toodle Lou's sells? Specifically the prices?"

"Yes, Hillary."

"And you see all the customers waiting to come in."

"I can hardly ignore them, Hillary."

She swallowed. "Well, from here, you can watch the business Toodle Lou's does and the age of the Toodle Lou customer. Incidentally, Moon Shadows is being sold here tonight." Hillary pointed to the display by the front cash register and signaled a white-jacketed waiter discreetly waiting to one side. He immediately brought them tropical drinks, the kind with tiny umbrellas and big price tags. Too bad the mall restaurant hadn't wanted a custom-blended perfume. They had preferred dollars to scents.

As Paul carefully fished out his umbrella, Hillary wondered if she had overdone the ambiance a bit. She hadn't realized how close to the window people would stand, or how many would stare at them.

But Paul didn't once comment on their surroundings. He was a charming continental dinner partner, at ease, even though they were on display for anyone wandering by.

"Is that real food?"

Startled, Hillary looked at a woman whose head was level with the table. "Yes."

"Are you going to eat your roll?"

Hillary opened her mouth, but couldn't think of anything to say.

"Allow me." Paul plucked his own roll from the plate and stooped to offer it to a fussy toddler strapped in a stroller. The child's whining, unnoticed by Hillary until that moment, stopped immediately.

"Thanks." The mother smiled.

"Not at all." Paul's answering smile caused the woman to blush.

Unruffled, he returned to his meal, apparently more comfortable than Hillary, who had lost her appetite. It was just as well, she thought as another hand reached for her roll.

"I got the last one, huh?" observed somebody's amiable boyfriend.

"Looks like it." Hillary managed a smile.

"Y'all giving out fish samples, too?" He gestured toward the rapidly cooling red snapper on Hillary's plate.

She shot a desperate glance toward Paul, then back to the boyfriend. "It's...it's plastic," she said through her teeth.

"Rubbery," Paul murmured. "But well seasoned."

The roll filcher touched the fish as Hillary stared in dismay. "Gosh, it feels real. They're getting good with that stuff." He nodded and wandered off.

"Hillary, Hillary." Paul clicked his tongue. "The fish *is* overcooked—but plastic? There's no need to insult the chef."

Paul was a good sport, Hillary thought, but he wasn't terribly impressed.

Sometime after the fish, but before the sorbet, Moon Shadows sold out. Once this was accomplished, Hillary relaxed, but refrained from pointing out the empty tray to Paul.

"I would like to know more about you, Hillary. Why do you do what you do?"

Sometimes she wondered herself. At least Paul was still speaking to her. "You want to know how I became a perfumer?" she asked, choosing the easiest interpretation of his question.

Paul inclined his head and spread his hands.

Hillary twirled the fuchsia umbrella she had saved from her drink. "I learned in a commune."

Paul blinked. "I can't picture you as a religious fanatic."

"Nothing like that. Just a group of people who wanted to live off the land."

Paul leaned forward, smiling slightly. "That still doesn't sound like you."

Hillary fiddled with the umbrella. "Typical teenage rebellion, something to annoy my parents. I met my partner, Melody, at the commune."

"I wondered. You two are not at all alike."

"She made the soaps and potpourris the commune sold. I got assigned to her and she taught me. I loved mixing lotions and soaps and I was good at it."

"But you left the commune?"

"Living there wasn't any fun if it didn't bother my parents." Hillary began to laugh as she remembered. "They said they admired me for living according to my values. Here I was, no electricity, no running water, and they encouraged me!"

Paul joined in her laughter. "Your parents were very clever. What finally happened?"

"Melody's son had an earache and herbs weren't helping. She wanted to take him to a doctor, but the leaders objected to the use of conventional medicines. She and her husband decided to go, anyway, and they were told not to come back. They headed east to Houston—everybody was at that time—and I came with them."

"And then, you joined together and opened your store?"

Hillary nodded. "Where Earth Scents is now."

"And your perfume training?"

"I *loved* experimenting with scents, so for my twenty-first birthday, my family sent me to France and I studied perfume at a fragrance laboratory. Or rather, I worked on increasing my olfactory memory."

"I had no idea you'd studied in France." Paul looked impressed, which wasn't entirely warranted.

"Just a few weeks—not the years I should have studied." *And could have, if I spoke better French,* she added silently. "But I learned enough to continue memorizing scents."

"Our perfumer keeps a notebook with his impressions," Paul commented.

"So do I." Hillary smiled before confiding, "Each time I smell a new ingredient, I feel this . . . rush of emotion." Her hand fluttered as she attempted to explain.

"Your work means a great deal to you." Paul sat back in the wicker chair. His teeth teased his lower lip as he studied her.

"It's your turn," Hillary said, not comfortable with Paul's scrutiny. "For a Frenchman, you speak awfully good English."

A corner of Paul's mouth tilted upward. "In France, they tell me I speak awfully good French for an American. My parents divorced when I was very young. My mother is American and I lived with her and went to school in Philadelphia."

"But—"

"France is my home now." Paul clearly didn't want to discuss himself. "I would like to talk with you about another matter," he said, cutting off any further questions. "May we return to your lab?" The expression on his face was completely different from the faintly indulgent one he usually adopted with her.

Business, she thought, her heart beginning to pound. Her demonstration had worked! She must have persuaded him to buy her perfumes! He'd seen how well Moon Shadow sold. He'd seen that she could creatively market her product and she must have convinced him of her ability as a perfumer.

Paul stood to help her out of the display window. Hillary grasped the sheer fabric of the dress she'd borrowed. "Let me change first." She tried not to sound breathless and excited.

Hillary restrained herself from questioning Paul as they walked back to Scentsations. He strode immediately into her lab and picked up one of Hillary's copies of the Dominique perfume, sniffed it and nodded. "Your copies are quite good, you know. In some cases you improve the original. An artist must be careful when he—or she—" he nodded to Hillary "—copies so much she can't create her own."

"I don't—"

Paul waved away her words impatiently. "That isn't what I wanted to discuss with you. Dominique is a competitor of ours. As you know, St. Etienne hasn't released a new perfume in several years."

"Several decades," Hillary inserted and wished she hadn't.

"This," Paul continued repressively, motioning with the vial, "was a private St. Etienne perfume."

"They're scooping you, huh? So release it first."

"Dominique has recently... acquired the formula." He appeared to choose his words carefully.

"Acquired how?"

"It doesn't matter." His tone warned against further questions.

"If the formula was commissioned, then the owner can do with it as she pleases," Hillary pointed out. "Anyway, your perfumer must have kept a copy."

"Well, he didn't!" Paul said almost angrily. "So now Dominique has the formula and they're ready to launch."

"Then why don't they?"

"They will, unless St. Etienne agrees to the merger."

"Which you don't want." Hillary studied his angry face. "Dominique has a young, kicky sort of reputation. This perfume isn't their usual style. In fact, you represent opposite ends of the fashion industry." Hillary swallowed. "You have the reputation and the stature. Dominique has money and enthusiasm and youth. I know they've been trying to upgrade their image. Much as it pains me to say it, a merger sounds like the best thing for both of you."

"Never!" Paul snapped, then took a deep breath. "Never," he repeated.

Hillary was too relieved to question his decision, not that she had any right to. "So you see? You *need* my perfumes! *They're* ready to go. Dominique releases a classic traditional. You release a young, modern scent. Beat Dominique at their own game!"

Paul's face softened. "I can't."

Disappointment shot through her. "You mean you won't."

"Hillary, insiders claim that the last major perfume launched by a couturier cost forty million dollars. Forty million. That's beyond the resources of St. Etienne."

Hillary guessed that the admission hadn't been easy to make. She knew that, for years, St. Etienne had depended on word of mouth and an occasional discreet notice in fashion magazines. Exclusivity was its hallmark, and St. Etienne won customers from the two thousand or so women who patronized made-to-measure designers. Volitaire and Sainte were two enduring classic perfumes, but their popularity was dwindling, as was the number of St. Etienne clients. Now that she thought about it, Hillary rarely saw St. Etienne clothes featured in fashion magazines.

Of course the company was entirely owned by the St. Etienne family. With no stockholders to answer to, they could presumably do as they wished. If they didn't want to change with the times, they didn't have to. But how she'd love to make them a presentation! "I'm not asking for a forty-million dollar launch." She wasn't ready to give up yet.

Paul sat next to her at the organ and took both her hands in his. "You've got talent. A raw talent. Perhaps after some further study, you would wish to make changes to your perfumes. Say, a more mature scent? Heavier, more complex?"

"You mean more like a St. Etienne perfume?" Hillary withdrew her hands. "I've spent several years experimenting with these perfumes. I didn't mix them this morning, you know." Now she picked her words carefully, not wanting to alienate Paul. "Would it be possible for me to make a presentation to the St. Etienne family?"

Paul threw back his head and laughed. Laughed just long enough to make Hillary wonder if he were approaching hysteria.

"Ah, if we could bottle your determination, Hillary, we'd all be rich."

She narrowed her eyes. Short people were patronized a lot. Young blond women with wide green eyes were considered mental lightweights. Inside Hillary's blond beach-bunny body lurked a savvy, sultry brunette. A *tall* savvy, sultry brunette.

"You're angry," Paul said, leaning forward. "Please don't be. I do have a favor to ask." His expression was appealingly earnest.

Hillary was only slightly mollified. "What?"

Paul closed his eyes for a moment. "The Dominique woman has become most annoying."

"Is she a brunette?"

"I beg your pardon?"

Hillary shook her head. "Never mind. Go on."

"I want to copy this perfume. It only needs to be good enough to fool someone who's untrained."

"Why doesn't your perfumer mix the copy?"

"You've already made a start and you have the chemical analysis." He tilted his head and gave her a half smile. "And, I think, you would welcome the challenge."

"Why do you want a copy when you have a sample?" Had Paul been responsible for the formula and didn't want to admit to the St. Etienne family that he had lost it? Or was this strictly an audition?

Paul hesitated. "I wish to commission a perfume—this one—from Scentsations. Must you know my reasons?"

Of course not. Hillary turned away to pick up some forms in an effort to hide the pink flush of embarrassment in her cheeks. "One moment," she said, "and I'll give you an estimate. What quantity?" Her face now a professional mask, she sat with her pen held above the carbonless form.

Paul reached for the pen and slipped it from her fingers. He met Hillary's questioning gaze with a handsome-Frenchman-caught-in-an-appealing-naughtiness smile. "Don't be angry with me."

Look at those eyes, Hillary admonished herself, noting how the corners crinkled. *And that mouth, curving just enough to hint at some little-boy dimples.* He'd certainly had a lot of practice using that look. Probably perfected it in front of a mirror.

She was immune. "I have nothing to be angry about, do I?"

"A smile then?" he asked coaxingly, widening his own.

She was *not* some little girl. She was *not* a gullible unsophisticated American. She was *not* going to smile.

She smiled.

"I'm embarrassed, you see," he told her. "The Dominique woman is so..."

"Annoyingly persistent," Hillary supplied.

"And makes me so..."

"Frustrated."

"That I want to..."

"Send her a whole gallon of the stuff in a gorgeous bottle with a slow leak?"

"Exactly!"

So, Paul was not above a few tricks of his own. They grinned at each other in perfect understanding.

"I can arrange that. It'll be fun."

"Good." Paul pushed back from the table. "You will need some time. I realize I can't expect an exact copy. Do the best you can in, say, a week?"

Hillary nodded.

"I'll schedule visits to the other North American St. Etienne boutiques. Locate the most impressive bottle you can."

Just because she agreed to copy his perfume didn't mean she'd given up on selling him her own, but she was in support of anything that would keep the Dominique hussy away from him.

And then what? Would she ever see him again?

Paul was standing once more and Hillary realized that if she didn't say something, the next word he spoke would be "goodbye." She didn't want him to say goodbye yet. She needed more time to convince him that St. E would benefit from a youth injection.

The appeal of Paul as a man had nothing to do with anything.

She grabbed for Dominique's liquid sample. "This has got civet in it. I don't use civet as a fixative. It's a secretion collected from a gland in a type of Ethiopian cat. The gland is irritated to increase production, and it's painful for the cat, so I won't use civet."

Paul's expression indicated that he'd already been thinking of something else. "I suppose you don't wear furs, either."

At least he gave her credit for her convictions and not the fact that she couldn't afford a fur. "No, I don't." She tilted her head self-righteously and then spoiled it. "Besides, fur season in Houston is about three days long."

Paul looked down at her and smiled gently. She knew he'd probably guessed that she was talking only to keep him with her. "Will it bother you if I sit here and watch?"

Yes, it would bother her and, no, she wasn't going to tell him. "Have a seat."

"I'm sure there are some synthetic fixatives that capture civet's leathery smell as effectively," Paul said as he sat next to her organ.

"Yes, but I wanted you to know because it will make a difference."

Hillary began mixing and blotting and sniffing. "Where are the St. Etienne boutiques?"

"Let's see. Montreal, Palm Beach, Scottsdale and Miami. That's where most of our clients are."

Hillary didn't say anything. Except for Montreal, they all had sizable retirement communities.

"We also have larger boutiques in Hong Kong and Abu Dhabi."

"Impressive."

Paul shrugged. "The Saudis like the ornate brocades we use for our evening clothes."

And they'd love the heavy perfume I'm copying, too, Hillary thought. Aloud she said, "I thought the women had to wear black sacks."

"They wear our clothes under the *abaya,*" Paul said dryly.

"Not so great for your designers' egos."

"They are well paid."

His terse remark warned her to change the subject. She handed him a blotter. "What do you think of this so far?"

Paul sniffed. "The essence is there for a moment, but the *note de coeur,* the basic fragrance, is lacking, I think. You have a natural gift."

"Just a knack for scents. My nose is like anyone else's."

"You have a very charming nose."

"I've simply had some training," Hillary said with a quelling look.

"Have you ever considered more training?"

Hillary toyed with the blotters before answering. "Yes," she said slowly, "if I thought it would help my career."

"You should apprentice yourself to one of the houses. Then you could land a job anywhere."

"I *have* a job."

"I meant as a perfumer. Say for one of the fragrance labs."

"I already am a perfumer." Hillary threw the blotters onto her desk in exasperation. "Why would I want to work for anyone else? Most perfumers are at chemical houses. And my life's goal isn't to create a new pine scent that can be scratched and sniffed in the Sunday coupon supplements. I love perfume. Everything about it. Not just the scent. The whole thing is a magical fantasy that you create and bottle."

Paul leaned forward. "Then think of the opportunities you would have as a perfumer to a great house."

"I know! So I'm trying to make this house—Scentsations—a great house." Hillary tilted her chin. "Some day, I might compete with St. Etienne."

"Yes," Paul said, his voice expressionless. "Some day you might." He stood, looking down at her for endless moments. "Au revoir, Hillary."

CHAPTER FIVE

SHE MISSED HIM. She told herself she hadn't known him long enough to miss him. Maybe she didn't actually miss him. Maybe she only missed the way he made all five feet one inch of her feel sultry and womanly.

Paul wasn't due back for several days, but Hillary wanted to have the perfume copy ready. She stared at the small rack of vials containing her perfume mixtures, all pale imitations of that Dominique woman's heavy, overblown scent. First she'd get the cheaper ingredients right, then she'd experiment with the expensive stuff.

"Hillary?" Melody carried a large box into the lab. "Take a look at these bottles."

"What have you got?" Hillary, glad of the break, eyed Melody and groaned inwardly.

Today was Melody's turn at Scentsations. She wore a slim black skirt and long-sleeved white blouse, her attempt at elegance. Her long hair was bunched in a barrette at the nape of her neck, and its rippled frizziness lay like a pelt on her back. Melody wore flats without stockings and no makeup. She was as out of place at Scentsations as Hillary was at Earth Scents.

"This is the biggest bottle." Melody hefted a square jar, vaguely reminiscent of the beautifully classic Chanel N° 5 bottle.

"No." Hillary shook her head. "I wanted something bigger."

"Bigger than a quart?"

"Yes...That's more like it!" Hillary pointed to a jug by the door.

Melody turned to look. "Hillary, that's the Ozark Springs water bottle."

"It's about the right size."

Melody studied the thick, bluish glass jug. "There isn't a cap. We'd have to make one and it would probably leak."

Hillary grinned. "What a pity."

Melody looked confused. "Well, Natasha could pretty it up, maybe glue some jewels and sequins..."

She trailed off as Hillary winced at the horror of a five-gallon Ozark Springs jug prettied up.

"Let's try for a gallon size," Hillary suggested.

"Apple juice," Melody said promptly. "We can buy a gallon of apple juice and use the bottle."

"No." But Hillary wasn't quick enough. She knew Melody was already thinking about recycling apple-juice jugs and filling them with one homey lotion or another. "Melody, people aren't going to buy moisturizer by the gallon."

"We wouldn't have to charge as much since we didn't pay for the bottle," Melody said, confirming Hillary's suspicions.

"Uh, wouldn't it be kind of heavy?"

"Oh, no, Hillary, our moisturizers are light. Heavy ones clog pores."

In another person, her comment would have been sarcastic. Unfortunately Melody was completely, if naively, serious. She pawed through the other candidates for the Dominique bottle. "Too bad a glassblower can't make you a bottle. Then you could have exactly what you want."

"Know any glassblowers?" Hillary asked, unable to keep the impatience from her voice.

Melody nodded. "Just the man at the Renaissance Festival. He lives at the site all year. Some lucky people do."

"Melody!" Hillary grabbed her friend by the arm. "You're brilliant!"

"I already called him," Melody said, shaking her head. "He said if he made a bottle like the one you want, the shoulders would be weak. And if someone jammed the stopper into it, like if they weren't really, really careful, the neck would break."

"Break?" Hillary asked with a wide smile.

"Uh-huh. So that won't work, either."

"*Au contraire.* It's perfect." Hillary grabbed the phone on her desk. "What's his number?"

"What are you going to do?" Suspicion shaded Melody's voice as she dug in her wallet for the glassblower's phone number.

"Remember what Josephine did when Napoleon ditched her?"

Melody sorted through business cards. "Not off the top of my head."

"She saturated the imperial apartments in musk. Not only did Napoleon hate musk, it's one of the longest-lasting scents."

"So?" Alarm widened Melody's eyes.

Hillary took the dog-eared business card Melody handed her. "So, thanks to the wonders of modern chemistry, there's going to be a lot of musk in that bottle."

She could hardly wait for Paul's return. The glassblower delivered a beautiful bottle with a milk-glass rose stopper. Incorporating the St. Etienne logo was an in-

spired touch, Hillary thought. When the Dominique
woman shattered the fragile bottle—Hillary could just
picture her jamming the stopper back in annoyance—the
St. Etienne white rose would be left to mock her as she
tried to escape the overpowering stench of a sea of perfume.

Every time she worked with the sample, Hillary was
reminded of Paul's hotel room and her anger rekindled.
Dominique's perfume was destined to become one of the
great classics, and if Hillary hadn't been angry, she
might have been jealous. The blend of scents was a little
old-fashioned but would appeal to the St. Etienne customers, since they liked the unchanging line of traditional, bordering on dowdy, clothes. Was Dominique
trying to poach the St. Etienne devotee?

The thought depressed her. She loved her perfumes,
Sun Shimmers and Moon Shadows. They were for active women, women who played tennis and possessed
aerobically honed thighs. Dominique women.

Maybe she could meet someone with St. Etienne who
wasn't as obstinately opposed, as Paul was, to joining
the nineties.

Hillary had been thinking of him so much she was
hardly surprised when he called.

"How goes the fabulous fake?" He sounded light-
hearted.

"I'm almost ready to add the expensive oils," Hillary told him, irrationally disappointed that he hadn't
asked about her first.

"Looks like you'll have a few more days. I'm snowed
in."

Hillary's eyebrows raised. "Where? Palm Beach or
Miami?"

Paul laughed his uninhibited laugh. "Hillary, you're good for me. I'm back in Montreal battling an unseasonably early snow. Flight schedules are a mess."

He couldn't be much older than she. Why did he adopt such a worldly, avuncular attitude toward her? She'd hoped Paul would see beneath her blond, freckled exterior and take her seriously. "I hope you're having a good time jaunting about. I've been working hard getting ready for the Christmas onslaught."

"As have I. We'll play when I return to Houston."

She should squash this right now. *Right now.* Paul was great flirting material. However, when he flirted, he didn't think about her perfumes. Until any possibility of her selling to St. Etienne was over, there should be no flirting.

"Now Paul, you know retailers can't play during the shopping frenzy."

"That's the best time to play. You choose the game—"

"Paul..."

"Or I will. Bye."

She heard the click, yet listened for a few more seconds, tapping her nails on the receiver before hanging up. It didn't look as though Paul would ever seriously consider her perfumes, which left her nearly where she was a year ago. An unknown.

Suddenly Hillary didn't want to spend any more time copying Dominique's perfume. Walking to the front of the store, she admired the glinting crystal housing her own perfumes. Natasha, in spite of an exuberantly casual attitude toward her first job, didn't allow even a day's worth of dust to dim the sparkling glass.

As Hillary sat behind the counter, she considered removing her suit jacket or dimming the bright lights, their

extra heat being the price she paid to show off the jew-
ellike facets of the bottles.

"Hey, she's finally going to come in," Natasha said,
gesturing toward the door.

An elegantly suited woman with a cap of dark hair
walked through the Scentsations entrance. Hillary re-
buttoned her jacket.

"She's been by here, staring in, at least three times,"
Natasha whispered.

"Shh," Hillary said automatically. She didn't get up
from her seat behind the counter. One didn't pounce on
one's customers.

To her surprise the woman, after a brief glance at
Natasha, ignored the inviting displays of perfumes,
bottles, sachets and bath oils and walked directly to
Hillary. "You must be the owner," the woman said with
a confident smile.

Hillary nodded, matching her pearly white for pearly
white. "I'm Hillary Simpson."

"Caroline Waite." The woman extended her hand. "I
could just tell you were in charge."

If someone other than a tall, impeccably clad brunette—Hillary, for instance—had said that, it would
have been gushy. Svelte brunettes could get away with a
lot.

"How may I help you?" Hillary asked in her impor-
tant-person-conversing-with-a-peer voice.

"I think it's more a matter of how we can help each
other," the woman stated. The commas on either side of
her mouth deepened.

Hillary rapidly reviewed every name in memory. Caroline Waite. Nothing. "In what way?"

Caroline blinked. "Paul hasn't mentioned me?"

Hillary bit back a retort. Paul had not mentioned Caroline. Hillary didn't have the faintest idea who she was. And now that Hillary had hesitated, Caroline must realize it. "No," Hillary admitted, anyway, and forced a faintly regretful smile to her lips.

She saw surprise, and something very like relief, reflected in Caroline's eyes.

Hillary didn't know what to say next. She could hear the muted mall traffic and the clinking of glass against glass as Natasha polished perfume bottles.

Caroline finally spoke. "Oh dear. Perhaps I shouldn't have..." She bit her lower lip and placed perfectly manicured fingers on Hillary's arm. "Please don't tell anyone I've been here. I didn't realize that Paul...my, this is awkward." Her laugh sounded embarrassed. "I don't suppose we could just say I stopped by for a perfume?"

"I don't see why not. After all, how do I know you didn't?" Hillary wasn't willing to make enemies unnecessarily.

"Oh, thank you." Caroline gave Hillary a brilliant smile.

"How do you know Paul?" Hillary asked, trying not to sound suspicious. Or jealous.

"We...we work together." Caroline was looking down at the display of fabulous fakes as she spoke.

This woman and Paul worked together? The thought made Hillary's teeth hurt. Especially since Paul had neglected to mention Caroline.

"Do you only sell copies?" Caroline asked, picking up a tester.

"And a few house perfumes." Hillary hesitated, then withdrew two tiny vials from a precious hoard underneath the counter. "These are two of our popular house perfumes, Sun Shimmers and Moon Shadows. We also custom blend.''

As she'd hoped, Caroline put down the tester to sample the two scents.

Caroline was chic and sophisticated, not at all like the traditional St. Etienne woman. And, Hillary would be willing to bet, Caroline was not wearing a St. Etienne design. Her knees were showing; St. E never showed a knee.

Caroline replaced the tiny stoppers. ''These are lovely,'' she said, placing the samples in her pocket.

''Thank you.'' As Hillary recited the special qualities of her perfumes, she thought that Caroline was precisely the type of woman St. E should target. Perhaps if Caroline liked the perfumes, she could persuade Paul to buy them.

''Custom blending,'' Caroline read from the discreetly placed price list. ''Do you know, I've never had a perfume custom blended for me?''

''You're in the right place.'' Hillary smiled, now intensely curious about Caroline's position at St. Etienne, but not quite certain how to discover what it was.

''Who blends your perfumes?''

''I do.''

''Of course.'' Caroline gave a little laugh. ''I should have known you were the perfumer. I would be honored to have a perfume created by you.''

You don't want to tell me the real reason you're here, thought Hillary. Maybe Paul had mentioned her and Caroline was supposed to evaluate Hillary in some way. Maybe this was another audition. She decided to treat it as such.

''Let's see how you like these mixtures,'' she said, sliding off the stool and gesturing to Caroline to take her place. She headed toward the smaller scent organ she kept in the front window. "First, I'm going to let you sample some accords."

"Accords?"

Hillary embarked on her standard sales pitch. "Blends of several individual odors representing the basic types of perfumes. We'll see what appeals to you." Hillary handed Caroline a paper blotter she dipped in the citrus vial.

Caroline rejected it, then floral. Hillary wondered whether she was being deliberately difficult.

"Couldn't I smell the individual ingredients?" Impatience tinged Caroline's voice.

"There are tens of thousands of scents," Hillary replied, thinking of the revolting odors some of the floral concretes and absolutes had before they were diluted. "I'll be working with raw materials when I blend your perfume." Hillary handed Caroline a blotter from the leather/animal group.

"Hmm. Smells sexy." She gave Hillary a woman-to-woman smile.

Hillary was reminded of Josephine saturating Napoleon's apartments with musk, an odor so penetrating it can't be washed off polished steel. She let Caroline sample a chypre type next.

"Ooh, yes." Caroline closed her eyes.

"That's a soft, warm, sweet scent, like Miss Dior. Now try another one."

Caroline sniffed. "Oh, I know this. I can smell the sandalwood. I'm not too crazy about sandalwood."

"Oriental. You know, Youth Dew, Shalimar, Opium, Tabu." Hillary was puzzled. "I'm surprised you don't like that accord, since the chypres appealed to you."

"Well, I don't!" Caroline snapped.

Hillary's astonishment must have shown in her face because Caroline moderated her voice. "Don't you have anything lighter?"

"Sun Shimmers, one of the samples in your pocket, is a light perfume," Hillary hinted as she handed Caroline a blotter from a blend representing the "green" group.

"Yes." Caroline inhaled. "Piney leaves. But I don't want to smell like room deodorant, either."

Hillary handed Caroline the last blotter, already mentally mixing an eclectic modern perfume for her. She wasn't surprised by Caroline's enthusiastic reaction to the aldehydic scents.

"I like that sharpness. Makes people notice, then back off," Caroline said, nodding.

"Like Chanel N° 5." Hillary separated the mixtures Caroline preferred. "Unusual combination. You want a perfume that'll hit them between the eyes and then come on soft."

Caroline stared at Hillary with an exaggerated expression of comical surprise. "Yes! Exactly! That's my personality. I wonder if there's been a study done by psychologists or psychiatrists on personality and scent preferences?"

"I'm sure there has," Hillary murmured, deciding that she didn't like Caroline. She suspected that the brunette was being patronizing and she wondered what she really wanted. "Did you plan to attend the seminar with Paul?" Hillary probed.

"Not this time."

Hillary forced herself to remain quiet in the hope that Caroline would offer something about her position with St. Etienne. Or even something about Paul's position.

"Tell me about the seminar," Caroline asked instead.

Nothing was dearer to Hillary's heart. She launched into an enthusiastic recital of her plans, embellishing as she went along. The fact that Paul had expressed only a vague interest and would be surprised to hear these plans did not deter her. She would hold the seminar with or without him. Of course, the seminar would be infinitely better with Paul's participation, and if she could impress Caroline, Caroline might say a few words to Paul on Hillary's behalf.

"You probably know that Paul has expressed an interest in backing the seminar," Hillary confided, gratified to see the momentary expression of surprise that crossed Caroline's face.

Caroline recovered immediately. "Oh, Paul." She laughed a little arpeggio type of laugh. "I suppose this is another of his whims." Her eyes flicked up and down Hillary.

Hillary did not like being called a whim. "We've begun making plans."

"Really?" Another arpeggio.

"Really." Hillary responded with an arpeggio of her own.

"Oh, that was really naughty of him." Caroline shook her head. "Hillary, you've done me a favor—let me do one for you. Don't expect any financial help from St. Etienne."

Hillary hadn't. "Why not?"

Caroline studied a fingernail. "Paul is really quite desperate for money." She glanced up.

Hillary didn't have time to hide her stunned expression. "But he's sponsoring a perfumer's grant! I'm going to have a contest in connection with the seminar and the winners will study at St. Etienne.''

Caroline's smile now held a tinge of pity. ''I don't know what Paul's promised you, but I assure you he won't be able to provide more than moral support. Sorry.''

Disappointment shot through her. Why would Paul make promises he couldn't keep? Or... A horrible thought occurred. Was Caroline Paul's superior? ''But he said he might release the winner's perfume.''

Caroline had a distant look in her eyes as she stared out the glass display window behind Hillary. ''What a beautiful publicity stunt,'' she murmured to herself.

Hillary didn't know if she had intended to speak aloud or not.

''Notice he said 'might,''' Caroline pointed out to her. ''St. Etienne is entirely family-owned. They're quite proud of that, and no outsider has ever risen very far in the company.''

What was she intimating? That Paul was making empty promises to lure Hillary onto the perfumers' equivalent of a casting couch?

''You're an outsider, aren't you?'' Hillary asked.

Caroline stood and tilted her head back, giving Hillary an excellent view of her nostrils. ''Not for long.''

CHAPTER SIX

"HE LIED TO ME!" Hillary burst out, belatedly checking to see if Melody had customers after disrupting the tranquility of Earth Scents. Bound by her promise not to mention Caroline's visit, Hillary's anger had fermented over the past two days.

Melody took one look at her furious partner and handed Hillary a wicker basket containing lace sachets. "They're filled with sweet cicely, mint, heather and chervil, to lift the spirit. Sounds as if yours could use some lifting. Tie ribbons for me, please?"

Hillary took a deep breath and collapsed on a packing crate. "Why did Paul lie to me?"

"Did he?" Melody asked quietly, calm as usual. "How?" She pointed to the pile of pastel ribbons on the antique sideboard next to Hillary.

Hillary scowled, grabbed a ribbon and threaded it through the lace. "It seems that St. Etienne is practically bankrupt. They can't afford to sponsor a grant. In fact, they probably can't afford Paul's ticket back to France!"

Melody appeared to think this over as she dusted three gallon-size apple-juice bottles filled with homemade apple moisturizer.

Hillary saw them and rolled her eyes, beginning to regret her impulsive visit to Earth Scents. It wasn't even her turn and she'd probably upset Melody, but if she couldn't discuss her churning feelings with someone, she'd explode.

She *liked* Paul. Their encounters left her invigorated, enthusiastic and alive. Although he was not a perfumer, he understood the creative process. His urbanity convinced her that she needed a bit of sophistication in her life. But Caroline's visit had spoiled it all for her. Paul's suavity now seemed smoothly calculated.

Besides, Hillary detested being bamboozled by anyone, even a handsome semi-Frenchman. Must be his American side.

"What happened? Did his check bounce?"

"Good question. I didn't ask him for one," Hillary admitted. "It seemed gauche with him going on about St. E boutiques in all the wealthy watering holes."

"You're always scolding me when I let some of my customers pay later," Melody pointed out.

"That's entirely different."

Melody raised an eyebrow and went back to her dusting.

"It is!" Elegant Paul St. Steven, a vice president at least, couldn't be compared with Melody's scruffy, and usually broke, college students. "All you have to do is pick up a phone and you can verify whether St. E has boutiques where Paul says they do."

The corner of Melody's mouth quirked in a half smile. "Which you did."

"Which I did," Hillary confessed. "St. E does have boutiques in all those places. Exclusive ones, which really means small and dinky."

Melody nodded as if she already knew. "Why wasn't his word good enough anymore?"

"Ha!" Hillary broke down and told Melody about the visit from Caroline Waite. She hadn't intended to, but Melody would be discreet.

"Hillary, you'd believe this woman rather than Paul? What does she do for St. Etienne, anyway?"

Hillary took a deep breath and finished tying a satin ribbon into a limp bow. "I never did find out."

Melody straightened from her dusting and threw Hillary a speaking look. "Then you don't really know anything at all, do you?" she said, her hands resting on her hips.

"No." Hillary grabbed a handful of ribbons and let them slither through her fingers.

"And what kind of employee divulges company secrets to a complete stranger? What if Paul really is considering buying your perfumes?"

"Then I'm glad I found out about his financial problems now!"

Melody sighed. "You're probably right."

The capitulation was so completely unexpected that it took a moment to register with Hillary.

"It's hardly a secret that St. Etienne has more reputation than substance," Melody continued, "but since the company is entirely family-owned, it isn't subject to the same government regulations as those trading on the stock exchange."

Hillary couldn't have been more surprised if Melody had begun speaking fluent Greek.

"It's also difficult to get complete profit figures, since privately owned firms aren't required to make financial statements public." Melody rearranged the smaller bottles on the shelves, their clinking and scraping the only sounds in the shop as astonishment rendered Hillary momentarily speechless.

"How do you know all this?" she finally managed to ask.

Melody looked at her in surprise. "Ben told me."

Her husband? "Ben studies the stock market?"

Melody nodded. "He uses his computer."

"Ben has a *computer?*" Hillary had forgotten all about the sachets.

"Yes," Melody confirmed impatiently, as if Hillary should already know. "I asked him about St. Etienne a few days ago. He said they didn't leave an electronic trail. Besides, they're based in France."

Hillary was still thinking about the computer. "If you've got a computer—"

"It's Ben's."

Hillary dismissed that with a wave. "Then why don't you computerize your bookkeeping?"

Melody gave her a blank look. "Because you handle all that, Hillary."

"I didn't know you had a computer." Hillary spoke very slowly and clearly.

"Ben bought the computer for the children and he's learning to use it, too."

"Why didn't you tell me?"

"Is it important?" Melody snapped. It was one of the few times Hillary had see a ripple in Melody's composure.

Hillary took a deep breath, erasing her own irritation. "I can teach Ben to do the bookkeeping for your shop," she explained. "It does take up quite a bit of my time."

Melody's frown smoothed. "That's because you always make things difficult."

Hillary thought of the hours she'd spent working with tax forms, a process complicated by Melody and Ben's casual bookkeeping.

"What do you think about the display change?" Melody's serenity was restored. "Instead of grouping by product, I've started grouping by fragrances. People have been buying more."

"They have? How much more?"

Melody's brow wrinkled. "I don't know—just more." She began refilling soap baskets.

"Well, how often do you have to restock?"

"I don't know!" A basket of raspberry soap fell to the floor. Pink balls rolled in all directions.

"I...I'm sorry." Melody bent to the floor and began gathering the soaps. Hillary, once she recovered from her surprise, joined her.

"I just get so flustered thinking about numbers," Melody said in an apologetic tone.

Melody never got flustered. "Then don't think about them." Hillary kept her voice soothingly matter-of-fact. "That's my job."

"But Ben says it shouldn't be. What if you make a big perfume deal with Paul? We can't expect you to baby-sit us financially forever."

"I'd never abandon you and Ben."

Melody slowly shook her head as she replaced the soap basket. "You don't owe us anything, Hillary."

"Yes, I do," Hillary insisted firmly. "You taught me so much. If I hadn't met you, I would never have discovered perfumery."

"And if it hadn't been for you, we'd never have been able to support ourselves doing what we loved."

Hillary looked at the sweet face of her friend and partner, her touchstone all these years. How would these gentle people survive if the partnership was dissolved?

"But you have dreams," Melody continued with a peculiar urgency. "And if Paul can make them come true, we don't want to stand in your way."

During the drive back to Scentsations, Hillary thought about what Melody had said. Dreams had a funny way of becoming nightmares. The only way she and Melody could afford to dissolve their partnership was if Melody and Ben became more businesslike. More aggressive.

More like her.

Hillary sighed. Melody wouldn't be Melody if she changed and Hillary didn't really want her to. Melody had found contentment.

But Hillary thrived on change. She welcomed challenges. She wanted to grow.

Unfortunately, taxes, utilities, supplies—everything—cost more than when they'd started their business nine years ago. Hillary sighed again. Maybe she should talk to Ben. His interest in computers might mean he was ready to take a more active part in the bookkeeping.

Hillary parked her car and walked the long way around the mall. She wanted to approach Scentsations from the front, the way customers would, so she could check the impression her store made next to the others. Was her display too understated? Did she need more flash? More glitter? What would attract the Christmas shopper?

She peered through the glass windows and stopped.

Behind the counter, over by the smaller organ in the window, an impeccably dressed Paul St. Steven dipped her blotters into perfume samples and presented them to two highly rouged women with blue-gray hair.

He was back. Hillary swallowed, her mouth suddenly dry. Even suspecting that he was—what were Caroline's words? *quite desperate for money*—couldn't tarnish Hillary's pleasure at seeing him again.

She'd forgotten that Paul was so good-looking. He wore his brown hair slightly longer than fashionable these days and she found she preferred it that way. Paul was not a pretty man, and surrounded by delicate crystal and feminine fripperies, he appeared very definitely male.

The happiness Hillary felt at seeing Paul again tempered her anger. After all, she *was* taking the word of a complete stranger before she'd talked to him.

Paul ducked his head, searching for something, and withdrew her order book. Was he actually going to write up an order? Where was Natasha? Hillary waited, but her assistant didn't emerge from the back.

Time for Hillary to intervene. Quickly walking into her shop, she had just a moment to appreciate what wonderful things a well-cut suit could do for a man's physique before Paul noticed her.

"Hello!" He greeted her with an enthusiastic smile. "I'm glad you're here." Was it her imagination, or did his words convey a deeper meaning? "Ladies, this is the perfumer, Hillary Simpson. She'll be able to answer any of your questions I didn't."

The women ignored her.

Professional mask in place, Hillary took her usual spot behind the counter and gently bumped Paul out of the way with her hip.

He bumped back and didn't move.

"You've decided on these scent bottles and you're choosing a perfume for them? Do you have a favorite fragrance?" Hillary asked.

"What do *you* like?" one of the women asked Paul, and tittered.

"I have my personal favorites." His voice—and his accent—deepened. He was going to tout Sainte or Volitaire, St. E's perfumes, she just knew it. He leaned toward the women, staring into their eyes. "Scents made memorable by the women who wore them."

Both ladies held their mouths in identical scarlet *O*'s. In Hillary's mind, a parade of sweetly scented seductresses tumbled in and out of Paul's waiting arms. Her own lips pressed together in a straight scarlet line.

"For instance," Paul picked up a vial and removed the stopper. The scent of gardenias wafted through the air. "My mother." He offered the vial to the two women.

One of them tapped his arm playfully. "You naughty man."

He was flirting with her customers! "Here's a sweet floral you might like." Hillary announced firmly, preparing to offer the women a whiff, but they had followed Paul to the other end of the counter to the fabulous-fakes display.

Hillary kept her eyes glued to the order book as the women continued to address Paul, relegating her to little more than his assistant. Though she was often mistaken for a salesclerk, she was usually able to shrug it off. But to have it happen in front of Paul, when she had tried so hard to burst his first impression of her as a bubble-brain, embarrassed her.

She knew it was silly, but her resentment built, nearly exploding when Paul offered the women the same floral she'd suggested—and they chose it. This was *her* shop. Surely Paul knew how she felt.

"Jot that down, would you Miss Simpson?" He was enjoying himself. The two women were enjoying themselves.

Hillary was not enjoying anything, especially the realization that she was the teensiest bit jealous of two women old enough to be her grandmothers. However, Hillary reminded herself virtuously, they were customers. So she jotted and Paul spritzed.

"Oh, they're all beginning to smell alike!" protested one woman.

"And we especially wanted to try that," the other said, pointing.

Sun Shimmers. Hillary smiled. To the virtuous go the spoils. Or was that the victor?

Without missing a beat, Paul shoved up the arm of his perfectly tailored sleeve, removed his platinum cuff link and rolled back a shirt cuff, then squirted his wrist. He waved it a moment, allowing the alcohol to evaporate, then offered his wrist to the women.

Giggling in unison, they also wrinkled their noses in unison. "Oh, no. That won't do at all."

Of course it wouldn't. Sun Shimmers was a woman's perfume, and Paul was unquestionably a man.

The women decided they were finished and Paul deftly wrapped their purchases, maintaining a cheerful salesman's patter and ending with, "Please come again."

There was a short silence as Hillary watched the women merge into the mall traffic. "You forgot to say, 'Have a nice day.'"

A smile lurked around the corners of Paul's mouth. "This is just a wild guess, but you're angry with me, aren't you?"

"I don't know yet. Where's Natasha?"

His forehead wrinkled. "Someone was having a sale."

"And she just left?" This was bad, even for Natasha.

"She said afternoons weren't a busy time of the day for you. The mothers are picking up their children from school and the business people aren't off work yet. I told her I'd watch the store if she wanted to shop." Paul's shrug was accompanied by his patented smile.

Hillary did not smile back. His actions clearly told her that he didn't take Scentsations—and by extension, Hillary Simpson—very seriously.

"I know," Paul said. "You're angry because those two ladies didn't treat you like the owner of the shop. Should they have saluted?"

"Don't patronize me." She donned her professional persona and slid off the stool, even though she was aware that standing didn't significantly increase her height.

"I would not presume to do so."

"Yet you do presume to interfere in my business."

The humor faded from his voice. "No harm was done. You're overreacting. This isn't my first stint as a salesclerk."

"That's not the point. Natasha is my employee," she stressed. "You are not."

Paul's expression told her that he was glad he wasn't. "You aren't going to fire her over this, are you?"

"That is not a matter for your concern."

Hillary saw the movement of the muscles in his jaw as he gritted his teeth. "Don't punish her because you're angry with me."

She kept her voice cool and unemotional. "If I walked into a St. Etienne boutique and told the sales staff to take a break, you'd fire them the moment they returned, wouldn't you?"

Hillary watched the heat slide into his cheeks and knew she'd made her point. Good. Just because Scentsations wasn't a behemoth like St. E didn't mean she had to put up with insults—or lies. "I have no intention of firing Natasha. She's an excellent saleswomen. Excellent. People not only buy, they feel good after having done so. But because she's young, she makes mistakes. As she did today." Hillary turned away, indicating that the conversation was at an end.

"Have I been dismissed?" The tone in his voice implied that she might have overdone it a bit.

Just as Hillary was wondering how she'd get herself out of this, Natasha breezed in. "Look what I bought at Toodle Lou's!" She held up a purple suede jacket. "Check out the fringe. Just because some of it got a little chewed on, Lou gave me seventy-five percent off! I'm going to cut the bad part into a heart shape and nobody'll ever know!" She admired her booty, looking up inquiringly at Hillary's lack of response.

"Uh-oh," Natasha said to Paul. "I thought you said she wouldn't mind."

"I was wrong."

"Yikes. Well, she never stays mad long. Are the scissors still in the back, Hillary?"

At Hillary's stiff nod, Natasha scampered into the lab, leaving the same awkwardness that had been there before her return.

"Now that Natasha is here, we can conclude our business." Hillary was aware that her words sounded stilted and formal. She thought she heard Paul sigh faintly.

"I suppose we can."

As she led the way into the back, Hillary was conscious of Paul behind her. "Natasha," she said to her irrepressible salesclerk, "we'll be in here discussing the perfume samples."

"Gotcha." Natasha formed a circle with her thumb and finger, shrugged on her jacket, admired her handiwork and strutted out to the front.

"Hillary." Paul reached out and touched her lightly on the shoulder, his hand spreading almost to the nape of her neck, which was exposed by her short businesswoman's haircut. She held herself rigidly, though her first reaction was to curl, catlike, toward him.

"I'm sorry. I was wrong." He added no excuses, nothing to dilute the strength of his apology.

"You meant well, I suppose."

"Ouch."

Hillary thawed. "It wasn't entirely your fault, I think. Natasha sold you on the idea. Selling is what she does best."

Paul made a small noise. "I don't know if I feel better or not."

Hillary smiled over her shoulder. "These perfumes will make you feel better." She hoped they would make *her* feel better. She hoped they'd remind Paul—and her—of her professional goals.

She directed him to the desk by her scent organ. "Here are four versions of Dominique's perfume." She gestured to the tiny vials. "There is one I prefer, but I wasn't able to copy the perfume exactly, even with the chromatograph reading. It's your choice."

Hillary left the room so Paul could relax and experience the mixtures. She was actually quite proud of them. Only an expert could distinguish the original from the imitations. Usually when she copied perfumes, there were subtle differences. People bought copies because they were less expensive than the originals. But cheaper oils smelled different, so she hadn't skimped on the fragrance oils in Dominique's perfume.

The ingredients for an ounce of the new Dominique perfume were fairly pricey to mix, compared with some. This perfume should have elegant and distinctive packaging and a bottle that was itself a work of art. Add to that the store markup, promotion and royalties, and Hillary guessed that the final cost to the consumer would be more than two hundred dollars an ounce. Almost half of that would be profit.

Hillary sighed again, nearly wishing she could be part of the Dominique launch team for this perfume. Had they named the fragrance yet?

Paul came to the doorway and held up a vial. "You didn't label these."

"Not necessary. Is that the one?" Hillary took a brief whiff and nodded. "My choice, as well. It doesn't have the staying power on skin that I'd like, but I'll compensate by mixing a stronger concentration of oils."

Paul stopped her from walking past, forcing her to stand next to him in the doorway. It was not a large doorway. "How do you do it? And so quickly?"

"Copy perfumes?" Hillary smiled a smile that told him she'd been asked this question before. "It's like orchestrating a symphony. You start with a melody. If the French horns play it, the music sounds different than if trumpets play it. Each instrument brings a different resonance to the melody. Perfumes are similar. I can derive scents several different ways. The trick is finding which one the perfumer used. Natural or synthetic? Perhaps a little of both?

"Now this one—" Hillary slipped past Paul and picked up the original Dominique fragrance "—must be an old formula. Several scents aren't used as often today, or there are chemical equivalents. This one didn't contain many synthetics."

"It was developed before the Second World War."

Hillary noted Paul's taut expression and changed the subject. "Let me show you the bottle."

She reached into a box filled with shredded paper. "I designed this with a glassblower. The bottle is an original, even if the perfume won't be."

She saw that Paul's attention was caught by the white St. Etienne rose on the stopper. "Beautiful." He turned to her. "St. Etienne doesn't have a bottle like that. We should."

Hillary winced. "Maybe not." She took a deep breath. "I have to tell you that the shoulders of the bottle are quite weak. If someone jammed in the stopper, the bottle would probably crack." Hillary watched for his reaction. "And, uh, all you'd have left would be a great big puddle and a white glass rose."

A slow smile grew across Paul's face as he grasped the significance of her warning. "I like you, Hillary." A twinkle lurked in the depths of his brown eyes. An unwilling chuckle escaped. "You really are quite delightful. We could work well together."

"That's what I've been trying to tell you. Just say the word, and Sun Shimmers and Moon Shadows become St. Etienne's newest releases." She held her breath.

Paul shook his head. "Not your perfumes, Hillary."

"Then are you offering me a job?" she asked flippantly, to cover her disappointment.

Paul studied her. "Would you accept one? We could dispense with the seminar and you could study at St. Etienne."

"I..." Hillary didn't know what to say. "It would have to be one heck of a job for me to give up Scentsations."

"But...St. Etienne..." Paul gestured expressively.

Yes, St. Etienne. According to Caroline, St. Etienne was on the skids. Even Melody, usually completely unaware of such matters, agreed that it was a possibility. Suppose Hillary considered the job—what could they afford to pay her?

"I make a good living from my store," she hinted.

"There is much more to success than money, as you surely know. A sterling reputation is worth more than gold." Paul smiled slightly at his play on words, unknowingly confirming Hillary's suspicions.

"But it won't put chocolate-chip cookies on the table."

Paul looked at her in amused exasperation. "You are ready for another challenge. I can sense it. You wish to make a name for yourself."

"Yes," Hillary agreed, "but would I get recognition at St. Etienne? Or would I be expected to imitate your style at the expense of my own?"

"Perfumers all over the world beg for a chance to work in the St. Etienne labs." Pride rang in Paul's voice.

Hillary put the white-rose-topped bottle back into its shredded paper nest. "Do you ever release any of their perfumes, or only those developed by your house perfumer?"

Paul bristled at Hillary's unappreciative attitude. "St. Etienne has high standards."

"Standards that no one but the famous Maurice St. Etienne has ever met." And not for a long time, Hillary added to herself.

Paul's eyes widened as he stared hard at her. "Perhaps," he began, then he paused, visibly banking his anger. "Perhaps we shouldn't work together, after all. Our association could take a different direction." His voice softened.

What an ego. He seemed to think he was doing her a favor by asking her to give up a perfectly good business to work for him. And probably for free. Hillary couldn't let him get away with that. "I think we'd work together just fine, Paul. But perhaps not at St. Etienne. You were a really great clerk this afternoon. Scentsations will need extra Christmas help. The job is yours, if you want it." She turned and leaned with her back to the table, folding her arms across her chest.

Now she'd done it. Paul's head reared like an angry stallion. "You have deliberately insulted me. If you do not wish to work at St. Etienne, a simple refusal will be adequate."

Hillary's voice rose. "I no more insulted you than you did me. *I* am part owner of my own company!"

"As am I!"

He suddenly sounded like more than a vice president. Hillary toned down her voice. "What do you mean?"

"I am St. Etienne."

CHAPTER SEVEN

HILLARY FELT HER MOUTH drop open and she shut it at once. She opened it again to say something, then closed it when she changed her mind, horribly aware that she probably reminded Paul of a gasping fish.

He shrugged apologetically, the naughty French-boy smile peeping out. "Most people connect the name, you see."

"But you said your name was Paul St.—" Hillary had found her voice, only to lose it once more.

"St. Steven, I know." He took a long breath, led Hillary to her workbench and drew a chair to one side. "It's a habit." He gently pushed Hillary into the chair, taking the stool for himself. "Since I was a young boy, I've always used the Anglicized version of my name when I'm in the United States. Young boys do so want to fit in."

Hillary remembered all the peculiar expressions she had seen flit across Paul's face. Now she understood them. "I know Etienne is French for Steven. I just thought if you were a *family* member you'd use Etienne. No wonder you think I'm a fluff-brain."

Paul laughed. "I find you charming and refreshing."

And hopelessly naive and provincial. "You should have told me!"

Paul's even white teeth tugged at his lower lip. "Hillary, you are a determined woman. How would you have treated me once you realized that Maurice St. Etienne was my grandfather?''

Hillary's mouth dropped open again and a laughing Paul gently closed it with his finger.

Suddenly she gave an agonized groan before burying her head in her lap.

"My seminar!" Her voice was muffled. "I could have had Maurice St. Etienne's grandson at my seminar and I blew it! I can't believe— The seminar could have been—" She broke off with another moan.

"Hillary?" She felt Paul's warm hand on her shoulder.

"I'm all right. Haven't you seen anybody wallow in self-pity before?"

"Not so enthusiastically."

She looked up to see him smiling at her.

"I promise I'll come back for your seminar."

"Promise?" Hillary heard the little-girl tone in her voice and wanted to bury her head again.

"Promise," he assured her gravely.

"I'm going to hold you to that," Hillary declared as she straightened and smoothed her hair.

"Good. I intend you to." He looked at her with a quizzical expression. "Am I forgiven, then?"

"There's nothing for me to forgive. *I'm* the one who was stupid." She moaned once more. "I can't believe I actually offered you a job!"

He made a small movement. "I might need one."

Dominique. "The merger?" Would they squeeze him out?

Paul nodded. "I...don't like the way Dominique does business." He smiled to himself. "And I've been rather vocal with my opinions."

Hillary swallowed, then figured that since Paul was still here, he wouldn't bolt at some plain speaking. "The grapevine says St. Etienne is in trouble."

"Sour grapes."

"Really?" Hillary tilted her head speculatively.

Paul heaved a weight-of-the-world sigh. "Not entirely."

She wanted Paul to confide in her. He sounded as if he'd like to. "I thought we were—" Hillary hesitated, searching for the right word, but there wasn't one "—friends. I'd like to hear about St. Etienne."

Paul's lips curved in a gentle smile. "Generally, when a woman asks me about St. Etienne, she is interested in the clothes, the designs, the inner world of a glamourous industry. But you, you want to know all about the challenges in running the corporation, the marketing decisions—everything. My own family is only interested when they receive their quarterly allowances, and then their main concern is why the checks aren't bigger. But they aren't interested enough to reinvest those checks in the company."

Hillary began to get a clearer picture of Paul's life. "You do, though, don't you? You reinvest your money."

He raised both eyebrows and shrugged slightly.

"I knew it," Hillary said.

"You're different from the women in my family," Paul said, changing the subject. "You have such...drive and tenacity. You're determined to be modern and independent—"

"Qualities St. Etienne doesn't admire in a woman," Hillary couldn't help interjecting.

"Don't confuse me with the company," Paul said, an admonishing tone in his voice.

"How does your grandfather feel about his family's lack of interest?"

"He doesn't know, and I intend to see that he never knows."

Hillary didn't like the expression on Paul's face. He looked at her as if she were a child whose naïveté prevented her from understanding. "I'm twenty-nine," she said abruptly.

"Why tell me that?"

"You treat me like a child. I'm short and I look young. I *am* short, but I'm not young," she explained. "They're not the same thing at all."

Paul seemed annoyed with himself. "Add another apology to my tab."

"I'm not keeping a list."

"Good."

Hillary sat back in her chair and studied him for a moment. "Mexican food," she said suddenly. "Lots of cheap Mexican food."

"Were we discussing dinner?" Paul was clearly bewildered.

Hillary laughed and pulled him to his feet. "When I'm down in the dumps, I eat either chocolate or Mexican food. You look like a Mexican food man to me."

"You said *cheap* Mexican food."

Hillary nodded. "And lots of it."

There was an unfamiliar expression on his face. "Hillary…" he began, at a loss for words. "Hillary, I'm not broke, not by any means."

"You'd better not be. Wait until you see the perfume bill." She grabbed her purse from the filing cabinet and took his arm. "Come on, Paul. You'll love this."

He flicked out the lights in the lab. "We're not eating in a window again, are we?"

Hillary made a face. "No. And I guarantee Dominique won't find us, either."

"Touché."

"So you do speak French. I was beginning to wonder."

Paul's grin made the corners of his eyes crinkle. He didn't look like the head of a struggling corporation and he didn't look particularly French at the moment, either.

Hillary merged into the freeway traffic and drove away from the ritzy mall to the suburbs on the west side of Houston.

"Just remember to keep nodding your head yes and you'll get a whole plateful of food," she advised, pulling into the parking lot of the restaurant.

"What if I don't want a whole plateful of food?" Paul, savoir faire in place, opened the door for her.

"It's obligatory on your first visit," Hillary informed him as she steered him past the piñatas, picante sauce, plastic snakes and Mexican candy to stand in the cafeteria line.

"Chili relleño?" the server asked as Hillary laughingly handed Paul a plastic tray and a napkin-wrapped silverware bundle from the stack.

"What?" Paul leaned forward to examine the contents of the pan.

"It's a deep-fried, cheese-stuffed green pepper," Hillary explained.

"Relleño?" the server repeated impatiently.

"Say yes, Paul. You're holding up the line."

He smiled and nodded.

"Just give us one of everything," Hillary instructed the servers and watched as their plates flew from hand to hand collecting refried beans, rice, tamales, four kinds of enchiladas, flautas, chalupas, tacos, red and green chili and guacamole.

They reached the end of the line and collected their stainless steel platters. Paul looked down at his tray. "You've eaten this and lived?"

Hillary borrowed one of Melody's serene smiles. "Thrived."

She led the way to a booth in a room with a garish multicolored mural depicting glorious moments in the defeat of the Alamo. "Food for the soul, as well."

Paul enthusiastically embraced Tex Mex.

"Even I, in the worst of my blue funks, have never eaten six sopaipillas at once before," Hillary said with admiration.

Paul licked honey off his fingers and flicked the switch on the sombrero lamp at their table. It signaled a smiling waitress, who obligingly filled their request for another plastic basket of the hot dessert pastries.

Hillary laughed and shook her head. "You're going to regret that."

"I'll worry tomorrow," Paul said, squeezing honey into the hollow he'd poked into yet another puffed square.

"Probably sooner." Hillary shifted in the vinyl booth and succumbed to another sopaipilla herself.

She was still picking leftover flakes off the pale green melamine plate when she caught Paul eyeing the sopaipilla basket.

"No way, José." She lit the sombrero, asking for two coffees when the waitress came.

"I can't move." Paul didn't look upset in the least.

Hillary nudged his coffee mug closer to him. "That's the idea."

Paul cradled the mug with both hands. They were solid and square. Strong hands. "So, now I'm to sing for my supper?"

"You haven't exactly held up your end of the conversation."

Paul chuckled. "I was going to confide in you earlier. I still might. Our...friendship has progressed very quickly. I don't have time for many friends," he added in a reflective tone.

"Women friends or friend friends?" Hillary wondered where Caroline fit in, but she wasn't about to mention her. She reminded herself that Caroline had asked her not to say anything, although her silence made her feel disloyal.

"I have many women friends." This was said with an arch of his eyebrow.

"Ah, yes." Hillary tried for nonchalance. "We did discuss that before."

"Jealous?" Paul grinned with satisfaction.

"Friends don't make remarks like that to each other." Hillary was serious, even though it would earn her a nomination for Miss Prissy of the Year.

Here came the smile. "I haven't decided whether I want you to be just a friend or something more than a friend."

How like a man, she thought, disgusted. "Hey, Paul, get with it. We're in the nineties. We can be both."

Paul only smiled. And Hillary realized what she'd said. If she could manage not to blush, she'd retain some of her shattered sophistication.

She blinked, knowing she'd never be able to outstare him.

He blinked back.

"It's your turn to say something," she said tightly.

Paul increased the wattage on his killer Frenchman smile, reached across the sticky table, took one of her hands and gently kissed the palm.

Hillary swallowed. He was only playing, but she couldn't convince her racing heart of that. If she became more than friends with Paul, what would happen when he returned to France? No. Absolutely not. She was very definitely out of her league.

Her palm still registered the gentle pressure of his lips. Her heart still raced. "You can't fool me. I know your stomach is full of sopaipillas."

Paul gave her an exasperated look. "They're only filling the spot left by my deflated ego." He released her hand. "We'll continue this another time. In all seriousness, I agree men and women should be friends with their lovers, but not lovers with their friends. And they should avoid doing business with either."

"No hanky-panky if we work together?" She was alternately fascinated and unnerved by Paul's compartmentalized view of relationships.

"For you, I'll make an exception."

But Hillary knew he wouldn't. He meant they weren't going to work together. At least he accepted her refusal to compromise her style. The thought didn't bring Hillary as much satisfaction as she'd hoped.

"Start singing, mister, or I'll cut off your sopaipilla supply."

"Your threat would be more effective if I hadn't just eaten three baskets full."

"But now that you've tasted them, the cravings start."

Paul burst into laughter, which Hillary had wanted him to do. As he momentarily forgot his private demons, the years etched into his face melted away. "I wish I had met you years ago," he said impulsively.

"I wasn't the same person years ago."

"I was," he said, looking pensive. "I've been running St. Etienne a long time."

"You aren't that old."

"Thirty-eight." He shook his head. "No one else in my family, except my grandfather, had the aptitude, training or interest." He leaned forward, as if explaining to Hillary clarified it for himself. "The family owns St. Etienne and the company has always supported them. But the family grew larger and I'm afraid they were indulged. They take from the company without giving back. And the expenses are increasing."

He drew a quick breath. It wasn't a sigh. Hillary could sense a torrent of words welling up, fighting to spill out. Apparently once Paul decided to confide, he held nothing back.

"We must make enormous changes in the way we do business." He sat back in the booth as if the confession had been wrenched from him.

"Then why don't you?"

"My grandfather. Such changes would kill him."

"He'd rather let one of the best-known French fashion houses die a lingering death than adapt to a changing world?"

"He doesn't know the company is dying!" Paul said in a fierce undertone. "He must never know."

"Paul..." Hillary stopped to consider her words. Did he really think his grandfather was completely ignorant of everything that happened at St. Etienne? Even though she didn't know Maurice, she felt sure he must suspect something was wrong.

Paul stopped her from continuing. "Actually, we did adapt. As our couture clientele aged, we made many dinner suits, and draped dresses, to disguise..." Paul gestured with his hands in an attempt to convey his meaning without using unflattering words.

Hillary wasn't so tactful. "Crepey arms and sagging busts."

Paul winced and looked at her sternly. "Yes. And we started using heavier fabrics, which appeal to elderly people who feel the cold more. We also designed fabrics for homes. Although we don't like to admit it, quite a few curtains and bedspreads originated at the St. Etienne mill."

"So St. Etienne is adapting." Hillary thought Paul had been very clever.

He nodded. "I convinced my grandfather that designing luxury fabrics would be a favor to clients. He doesn't know the extent of the favor."

"Is it fair to lie to him?" Hillary eyed Paul over the rim of her mug.

Rather than becoming angry, Paul nodded as he considered her words. "I've asked myself the same thing. But what purpose would be served by hurting him? The reality wouldn't change."

"But something else could. You'd be able to compete for a younger market. It'll be twenty years before the baby boomers are ready for your clothes."

"I know." Paul's hand edged toward the sopaipilla basket.

"Don't bother. Those will be cold now." Hillary whisked the basket out of reach. "They won't be worth the calories. Besides, I have questions."

"Questions? I've told you more than I've told..." He paused and said his next words slowly, as if he had only just realized their significance. "Than I've ever told anyone."

Afraid he would stop, Hillary hastened to reassure him. "That's because you're not used to dealing with brazen American women."

"Hillary, I'm only half-French."

"Which half?"

Hillary could see that he didn't quite know how to respond to her. She felt comfortable teasing him. She only got into trouble when he teased her.

"My paternal half," he said, with the amused exasperation she was beginning to see a lot.

"That's right, you said you lived with your mother. How old were you when your father died?"

Paul shook his head. "He didn't die."

"Then why isn't he running St. Etienne?"

Sighing, Paul looked at her. "You aren't one for subtlety, are you?"

"Subtlety wastes time."

"All right, then. My parents married very young, to the chagrin of both families, but I was already on the way. Less than two years after they met, they parted. I was born when my mother was seventeen and my father was nineteen. He is...an old-fashioned playboy. He cares for nothing but his own pleasure. I rarely see him."

The waitress came to their table, even though they hadn't lit the sombrero. "More coffee?"

"No, thanks," Hillary answered and began to slide out of the booth. Paul echoed her refusal and, with a mock look of longing at the sopaipillas, joined her.

"Your grandfather is really more your father, isn't he?" Hillary asked as she unlocked the door to her car.

"That wasn't hard for you to guess." Paul smiled. "Yes, my mother *insisted* I spend every summer with my father's people, as she put it. I hated the visits." He spoke flatly and without emotion.

"You live in France now."

Paul shifted in the bucket seat so that he faced Hillary as she drove back to his hotel. She flicked a quick glance at his face, which was alternately shadowed and illuminated by the passing streetlights. "I'm telling you all of this so you'll understand why I make some of the business decisions I do. I don't want pity or sympathy. Just understanding."

Hillary guiltily abandoned her mental image of Paul as a lost little boy only to resurrect it when he began speaking again. "My childhood sounds like the plot of a very bad movie," he said, and laughed. "At first, my mother took me to France, then I began making the trip by myself. I never knew who would meet me at the airport or when. My French was limited and when I got to the château, no one ever knew what to do with me. My father was never there." He laughed again. "And the irony was that my American stepbrother and stepsister resented my European 'vacations.' Did I mention that my mother remarried while I was gone one summer?"

They were at a stoplight, serenaded by the pounding rock music playing on the radio of the car in the next lane. Paul's profile was to her now, harsh and unsmiling. Hillary guessed he resented his mother more than his father, yet she felt his irresponsible father was more at fault. She supposed it didn't matter now. "No, you didn't."

"I didn't even come home to the same city. That's when I began using St. Steven."

A honk behind her alerted Hillary to the green light. "So you felt as if you didn't fit in anyplace."

"Until I wandered into the perfume lab and found my grandfather. We became close. He would tell me stories of his days in the French Resistance."

"He doesn't sound like a frail sort of person to me."

"He's not frail, but he is desperately proud. The company was nearly bankrupted during the war—the blockades kept us from getting the supplies we needed. He single-handedly rebuilt St. Etienne."

"Wait a minute. I thought he was the perfumer."

Several heartbeats passed before Paul replied. "He was injured during the war—a head injury. He won't talk about it, but there were several operations and he can't detect certain odors now."

St. Etienne's legendary perfumer was no more? Hillary nodded slowly as her mind reeled. "Anosmia—olfactory blind spots."

"Yes, though he admits nothing and won't allow us to hire a new perfumer—even as an assistant."

"So that's why there haven't been any new St. Etienne perfumes." And that explained Paul's despair when he learned there was to be no gathering of perfumers.

"None that he has allowed us to release."

"And perfume is where the money is now."

"Yes." Paul's voice was quiet, barely above a whisper.

Hillary was aware that he had just entrusted her with information that would be very valuable to St. Etienne's rivals, especially Dominique. He trusted her. She felt honored and extremely flattered. It could well be the greatest compliment she had ever received. She was determined to live up to his trust.

"The seminar grant," Hillary said, comprehension dawning. "You wanted to find a perfumer your grandfather could train as his successor. That way he'd never have to admit his disability, and you could release perfumes without your grandfather's getting hurt."

"Guilty. And St. Etienne can bask in the publicity."

"But surely the perfumer would discover—"

"Not necessarily," Paul interrupted. "Grandfather is very good at concealing his limitations. He fooled me for years."

"You aren't a perfumer," Hillary pointed out.

"But there have been others. If anyone guessed, they've not said."

"You auditioned me with Dominique's copy, didn't you?"

"Yes." Paul didn't add anything else.

But Hillary could figure out the rest for herself now. "And at the same time you hoped Dominique would think your grandfather had retained a copy of the formula, right?" She pulled into a parking space behind the taxis in front of Paul's hotel.

She was concentrating on parallel parking, which she avoided whenever possible, and didn't notice the silence at first. Paul watched her for a moment, then stared out the window.

Hillary turned off the ignition. "You want them to assume your grandfather mixed the perfume, don't you?"

Paul glanced back at her. "Would that bother you?"

"Are you kidding? Me, be mistaken for Maurice St. Etienne? I'm flattered, but not terribly optimistic."

Paul smiled. "Dominique will still wonder if we have the formula."

"You know," Hillary said, thinking aloud, "I meant to annoy Dominique, but if the bottle breaks, it will be hard for them to analyze the perfume and see how close I got."

Hillary saw Paul's white teeth flash in the lights from the hotel. "I know. And I know you're very good. My grandfather could make you great."

Hillary caught her breath. So tempting, to study with a legendary perfumer, even as he was now. She'd live in France. Near Paul. However... "I don't want to be another Maurice St. Etienne. I want to be a Hillary Simpson."

Paul leaned his head against the back of the seat. "I understand." His voice sounded as though he wished he didn't.

"But someone else would kill for a chance to study with your grandfather." Hillary felt the familiar excitement new ideas always sparked. "Together, we're going to find that perfumer."

Paul turned his head. "The seminar?"

"Yes! If we work with each other on this, we can hold one in a few months. You'll start reaping the publicity rewards long before!"

"You almost make me believe—"

"Can you stay in Houston a little longer?"

Paul sat straighter. "You're serious."

"You bet!"

Paul studied her a moment, then leaned across the space between the two bucket seats. In a move of exquisite finesse that Hillary knew would have been the envy of teenage boys everywhere, he kissed her.

Though their bodies were separated by the car's design, it was one heck of a kiss—an expert's kiss. Paul was a man who obviously enjoyed kissing for its own sake, not just as a prelude to greater intimacy. His warm, sculpted mouth explored hers, discovering and revealing.

As her hand crept to his shoulder, she felt the warmth of his skin, the slight roughness of his late-day beard. She tasted the bitterness of coffee and the faint sweetness of honey.

Headlights flashed and Paul drew back, but Hillary couldn't. She was shocked at her response. Every nerve she possessed had come alive at the first touch of his lips and demanded, screamed for, more of his kisses.

"You're like no woman I've ever met," Paul whispered before his mouth claimed hers again.

And he was like no man she had ever met. He redefined man. All other men could only aspire to be Paul. And Paul desired her. He moved in a world of beautiful sultry women, yet Hillary Simpson was in his arms.

For now.

Hillary didn't want to think; she only wanted to feel.

Paul cradled her face with his hands, gently stroking the sides of her neck with his fingers as his lips caressed hers.

Hillary shuddered and deeply regretted that they were in a small car with bucket seats in full view of the doorman, valet-parking attendants and the drivers of assorted airport limousines. A tiny sound of frustration vibrated in her throat.

Paul lifted his head slightly to look at her, one hand stealing around to the back of her neck, where his fingers toyed with the ends of her hair. "What's wrong?"

Hillary gulped a couple of quick breaths before answering. "What about your theories on business relationships?"

As his gaze roamed over her face, Paul's fingers continued to caress her neck, sending tingles down her spine. "I told you already—for you, I'll make an exception."

CHAPTER EIGHT

PAUL WAS COURTING HER. There was no other word for it. Rather than the casual American dates Hillary was used to, Paul employed the ritualized gestures of another generation. Charmed though she was, Hillary didn't know how to respond. Was he courting for real or for play?

During the following week, they planned the seminar. Paul was all business and Hillary was not. For instance, here she sat in her lab, mooning over Paul as he spoke on the telephone instead of composing text for the brochures as she should have been.

"If we have a firm commitment from International Oils and Essences, the mall management will allow a three-day exhibition." Paul twisted in the chair, saw Hillary looking at him and gave her a wink and a thumbs-up sign.

Hillary, stomach knotted with tension, weakly returned the gesture. Paul took more risks than she did. He was a master wheeler-dealer. The exhibition was his idea.

He spoke into the telephone. "Three booths on the corner?"

Hillary's stomach churned.

"I don't know... Let me check the diagrams." Paul reached for the latest issue of *Cosmopolitan* magazine and rippled the pages near the phone receiver. Hillary

closed her eyes and concentrated on keeping her breakfast down. Paul was bluffing. There were no plans.
There were no charts. And so far, no one had reserved
space.

"Tell you what, if I move Far Eastern Importers, you
can have their two. I'll throw in the corner for nothing
and you can have a block of six. But I need a firm commitment."

Hillary heard Paul's fingers snap and she opened her
eyes. He wore a huge grin. "Fine. I'll watch for the
courier."

He hung up the phone. "They said yes!"

Hillary exhaled. "What if they'd said no?"

He opened his arms and Hillary crossed the room. "I
would have called someone else." He drew her onto his
lap. "Your hands are like ice."

"You are incredible."

"I know." Paul pulled her arms around his neck and
held them there as he captured her mouth in a quick kiss.

A warming tingle spread through her all the way to her
previously chilly fingers. Much too soon, Paul urged her
off his lap. "Up. I've got to call Far Eastern and tell
them that if they're quick, they can have booth space
next to International Oils. Then we'll celebrate with
lunch."

Hillary slowly returned to the typewriter, shaken from
the effect of just one quick kiss. In fact, just the *thought*
of Paul's kisses quickened her pulse.

"Hillary! Far Eastern's coming. Let's postpone our
lunch. I want to keep up the momentum. Besides,
there'll be more to celebrate at dinner."

"I'll order sandwiches," Hillary offered, but Paul had
already begun punching out another phone number.

Smiling to herself, Hillary sent Natasha to the food court on the mall's lower level.

"DONE." PAUL CROSSED his arms over his chest. "I just filled the last available spaces next to the fountain. The mall management was impressed enough to delay the Country Craft show until after our seminar."

"I don't believe it." Hillary dropped the papers she was proofreading onto her lap. "It took you one day. I spent weeks on the phone last summer and didn't accomplish anything. The mall people wouldn't even return my calls."

"Envious?"

"Mmm. Someday I want *my* name to open doors that way."

Paul's satisfied smile faded. "It's worse when those doors shut in your face."

Hillary remembered his interview with Pavilion and wondered if that was one of the doors he meant. "This seminar will help us both, won't it?"

"Yes." Paul drew a deep breath. "But enough seminar for today. I have discovered the most wonderful little place..."

Hillary felt a flutter of anticipation. How did Paul find these enchanting restaurants? Even though she'd lived in Houston for years, Hillary had never heard of some of the little bistros and cafés. And when did he have time to find them?

Each night, after their long hours of work, Paul insisted that Hillary return home to relax and change, then he called for her, driving the sleek little car he'd leased.

And afterward, she would invite him into her apartment. He always declined—after kissing her so thoroughly that she couldn't sleep for hours. That didn't help when their day had to begin before dawn in order to contact people in Europe.

But not tonight. No more kiss-and-run. No more politely correct good-nights. Tonight Hillary didn't plan to be either correct or polite. By the time Paul walked her through the apartment complex to her door, Hillary's knees were shaking. Her hands fumbled with the key. Paul slipped it from her trembling fingers and unlocked her door.

And Hillary grabbed him, jerking him inside with more eagerness than finesse.

"Hey!" Paul caught himself from falling. "Is this a seduction?"

"I hope so," Hillary breathed, desire overshadowing embarrassment.

"Let's do it right, then." Paul swooped her into his arms, kicked the door shut and carried her through the dimness to her small sofa.

He set her on the soft plushness, leaning her back, then covering her body with his. His fingers traced her jaw and lower lip.

"Please," she whispered, achingly aware of his sturdy length against her.

She felt his breath caress her face an instant before his lips softly brushed her cheek, chin and the side of her neck.

Quivering, trembling, shaking—whatever she was doing—Hillary couldn't stop. "Paul!"

"Hmm?" he murmured next to her ear.

"Kiss me," she whimpered.

And then Paul's lips were on hers. The relief Hillary felt was short-lived.

She'd thought Paul had kissed her before—bone-melting moments of passion at the end of long days of work. Moments when they celebrated small triumphs and comforted each other over minor disappointments. Tender moments spent exploring a new friendship and moments of anticipation at what that friendship could become.

During their good-nights, Hillary had learned the taste of him, the feel of him and the little movements that made him gasp. She knew the shape of his mouth, the angle her head should tilt and how high she should stretch on her toes to fit as close to him as possible. He had learned about the sensitive hollows of her neck and had perfected the gentle kisses that could make her clutch at him and whisper his name with trembling abandon.

And yet... and yet Paul had always called a halt, his smile tender and tinged with regret.

Now she knew why. This kiss was different. This kiss transported their relationship to another level.

This kiss frightened Hillary.

Her hands loosened their grip on his shoulders. Her body stilled.

Paul lifted his head, the sound of his breathing loud in the darkened room.

He must think she was awful.

But he didn't. "You see," he whispered and even that sounded loud. "You see how it can be between us?"

"I—"

"Hush." Paul sat on the edge of the sofa and tugged her hand. "Think about tonight. You must make a decision soon. And remember, Hillary, with us, it will be all—or nothing."

ALL OR NOTHING. All or nothing.

Hillary worked at her display organ, but couldn't get those words out of her mind. She knew what nothing was. What was *all?*

Paul casually entered the shop and deposited a single perfect red rose on the glass counter in front of her. "Good morning." He smiled at her before turning to greet Melody. Hillary softly caught her breath, not breathing again until he walked into the lab.

She inhaled deeply, then gripped the counter as dizziness swept over her. Drat him, anyway. She absolutely would not fall in love with him. Is that what he meant by *all?*

Melody crossed her legs and twisted on the chrome-and-black stool behind the Scentsations counter and looked from the rose to Hillary's face. "There are twenty-one meals to eat during the week and I know of fourteen you've eaten with Paul. Is this serious?"

"Actually, there were also a few breakfasts on days when we got an early start." Hillary tried for a casual tone, glancing up at Melody to see if it worked. "Don't look at me like that! Some of the people we called about the seminar live in different time zones."

"Twilight zones?"

Hillary twirled the thornless rose. A decision. She couldn't make any kind of decision now.

"Sorry I'm late!" Natasha burst into the shop. "Ooh, how romantic!" she cooed, clasping her hands in a theatrical gesture that somehow looked completely natural. "It's just like in those old movies my mom rents! First there's the single rose, probably red, but it's hard to tell in black-and-white, then bunches—in a long box with a big bow and then ... I can't remember if the diamond necklace or the mink coat comes next." She shook her head. "But, anyway, then you have to go away with him to an island."

"Galveston?" Hillary asked.

Natasha giggled. "No, silly. One of those foreign places that have roulette wheels, and you can wear a prom dress and kiss the dice for good luck."

Hillary hoped Paul was on the telephone so he wouldn't hear Natasha. She had come awfully close to describing his suave, continental manner. Of course Hillary now knew what that manner of Paul's hid, didn't she? And she hadn't handled it very well, had she?

"Oh! I almost forgot. When the bunch of roses comes, be careful when you take them out of the box. Sometimes these guys hide an engagement ring there and you wouldn't want to lose it."

"Thanks for the warning."

"Are you going to marry him, Hillary?" Melody asked as Natasha bubbled up to a customer.

"Melodeeee!" Hillary hooked her toes under the shelves and leaned back on her stool to check if Paul was at the desk. "We're working together on the seminar, for Pete's sake! Besides, he hasn't mentioned marriage."

Melody glanced in the door of the lab as she slid off the black vinyl and crossed the shop to stand near the small scent organ. "That wouldn't stop you."

Hillary set the rose to one side. "We are only business associates."

Melody received this comment with a speculative look on her face. From past experience with that look, Hillary knew the next few minutes were going to be uncomfortable.

"He must like you an awful lot," Melody said, confirming Hillary's suspicions.

"And I like him. I thought you liked him, too."

"I do." Melody idly rearranged the perfume testers on the mirrored tray. "What happens when you finish the seminar plans? Does your—" she floundered for a word "—relationship continue?"

Hillary tried to outstare Melody before surrendering by covering her face with her hands. "I don't know!" she moaned.

"Do you think it might?"

Hillary moaned again.

"Do you want it to?"

Hillary dropped her hands. "Why are you asking me all these questions?"

From the expression on Melody's face, Hillary knew she'd roused her partner's mothering instincts. "Sometimes you get ahead of yourself. You jump in without considering all the consequences."

Hillary was shaking her head before Melody finished. "Not this time. This time I've done nothing but consider consequences." Especially since last night. She clasped her hands in her lap to keep from waving them around.

"How far have things progressed between you two?" Dismay sounded in Melody's voice.

"Well, we're not—we haven't..." Hillary gestured vaguely, feeling her face warm.

"Do you love him?"

"No!" The sharp word drew the stares of Natasha and her customer. Hillary sighed, her eyes closed. "Life would be so much simpler if I could fall in love with a member of the Houston Chamber of Commerce."

Hillary opened her eyes to find Melody eyeing her astutely. "It's too late, isn't it? You're already in love with him."

Hillary clenched her fist. "I refuse to give in—it won't work—I'll fight it."

"Why?" Melody wore a bewildered expression.

"Because...because think of what being in love would mean. When you love someone, you want to be... together."

"Is 'married' the word you're looking for?"

Hillary exhaled forcefully. "Okay, married. Where do you think we'd live? In my dinky little apartment? No way. We'd live in France in a great big drafty but eminently aristocratic château." Hillary began ticking off items on her fingers. "I'd give up my home, my friends, my country and my identity. Who would run Scentsations? Do you want to?"

Melody's apprehensive face answered for her.

"It's okay, Melody. Scentsations isn't your style."

"Maybe Natasha?" Melody offered in a hesitant voice.

Hillary shook her head. "What's the point? I love my store and I don't want to be an absentee owner. So let's talk about perfumes. He hates my perfumes. No," Hillary amended, trying to be fair, "he likes them, but they don't fit the St. E style. Sure, I'll compose other formulas, but they're not going to be the St. E style, either. For that matter, *I'm* not the St. E style."

"What woman under the age of seventy is?"

A slinky, sultry brunette. Caroline. The name popped into Hillary's mind. She took a deep breath. "An ex-model who'd set off those horrid old St. Etienne clothes. No, one who'd *inspire* the designer to create a new line. But me? I'd be stuck wearing those frumpy clothes because the wife of a St. Etienne couldn't possibly wear off-the-rack. And forget any other designers—" She broke off as Melody smothered a smile.

"I hate those clothes," Hillary grumbled.

A chuckle escaped Melody.

"Go ahead and laugh, but if we marry, I'd have to change and I wouldn't be *me* anymore. And then what happens? Who'd he be in love with then?"

Melody regarded her for a few seconds. "Maybe we're being a bit premature. Maybe...he isn't thinking of marriage," Melody hinted delicately.

Memories of the previous night scorched Hillary's thoughts. She spoke with certainty. "Paul's not going for a quick fling, which means he's either going to ride off into the sunset, or—"

"Take you with him," Melody supplied.

Hillary nodded. "We've nearly finished with the seminar plans. He won't stay here much longer." And then she'd have to make a decision. Hillary picked up the velvety red rose.

"I wonder," Melody mused. "There have been all the signs of a classic textbook courtship." She tweaked Hillary's rose. "And at the end of a classic textbook courtship comes a classic textbook proposal."

Hillary began to line up the perfume testers by height, spoiling Melody's arrangement. "I won't let that happen. I'm not going to fall in love with him, at least not until I've sold Sun Shimmers and Moon Shadows. I intend to use the seminar for contacts, too, you know."

Melody picked up a small bottle of Sun Shimmers and stared at the golden liquid. "The seminar isn't until next spring."

Hillary didn't need reminding. "It's my best shot at success. I have to try." With a wistful smile, she picked up the bottle containing her other perfume. The dark brown liquid gleamed.

Melody sighed and returned Sun Shimmers to the mirrored tray. "Love or career. Tough decision."

Hillary nudged Moon Shadows next to its counterpart. Was that the decision Paul meant she had to make? Love or career? All or nothing? Why did it suddenly look as if he'd have all and she'd have nothing?

THE BOX OF LONG-STEMMED red roses—with big bow—arrived the next morning.

"What did I tell you?" Natasha gave a little jump and clapped her hands together. "Don't forget to check the stems."

"Things haven't progressed that far, Natasha." But Hillary was careful as she slipped off the ribbon and lifted the box lid.

"Are you sure? That's a lot more than a dozen roses." Natasha started counting as Hillary searched for the card.

"'One for each day I've known you,'" Hillary read aloud.

"Twenty-eight," Natasha announced.

Any normal woman would be squealing with delight at the sight of twenty-eight red roses. Any normal woman wouldn't be suffering an attack of nerves like the one that held Hillary in its grip.

"The accepted thing to do is to put them in water," offered a deep voice.

"Paul!" Hillary gave him a wide smile, hoping it looked like an I'm-pleased-to-get-the-two-dozen-plus-roses smile. She didn't have one of those in her repertoire. "I don't think I've got anything here to do them justice."

"Try this." He set a clear fluted vase on the counter.

"You think of everything." One movie cliché for Paul, one verbal cliché for her.

"I've planned a special luncheon for us today." Paul glanced from the vase to the frozen smile Hillary knew was on her face. The word *decision* screamed in her mind. She wasn't ready.

He walked back to the lab and filled the vase with water.

Her heart seemed to lodge in her throat. She doubted she'd be able to eat any special luncheon. "Do we have time? I was thinking of another trip to the food court." She grabbed a handful of the roses and dropped them into the vase.

With a reproachful look, Paul took over the arranging of the flowers. Hillary couldn't see what he was doing that was any different from what she'd done, but the roses were now an opulent mass. She sighed. Another elegant trifle she should have learned—and could have learned if she hadn't been so busy convincing her mother that she didn't care about such things.

"What makes you think we aren't going to the food court?"

She gave him a look from underneath her eyelashes and he grinned. "Okay," he admitted, "I made reservations at the little crepe place, the one that has the chocolate creation you like."

Hillary nodded. If Mexican food didn't cheer her up, a chocolate crepe would.

A single rose waited for her at the table. It prompted a new wave of nervousness. Why couldn't this be a regular working lunch like the others she'd so enjoyed? Why did Paul have to spoil everything?

Hillary decided to skip any special luncheon food and go directly for the crepe.

Paul leaned forward to grasp one of her hands in his, stroking the soft underside of her wrist with his thumb. "Your skin is like the petal of that rose." His French accent was suspiciously more pronounced than she'd ever heard it.

Hillary's pulse began to pound, and not with anticipation. This whole scene was hokey and embarrassing. "Because it's all red?"

Paul didn't laugh, but gave her a wounded look like a bad actor in a "B" movie.

He released her hand as the waitress brought Hillary's chocolate crepe. For once, she didn't want it.

Paul had ordered espresso for himself, and now he sipped his coffee as she tried to force down the sticky richness of the crepe.

A small chink sounded as Paul set the tiny cup back into its saucer. He reached into the breast pocket of his jacket and withdrew a flat velvet box, placing it on the table in front of her.

Her stomach revolted, the last swallow of chocolate crepe lodged firmly at the back of her throat.

"A small token of my regard for you."

She couldn't stand it. Everything Natasha had predicted was coming true.

Hillary wiped her hands on the cloth napkin crumpled in her lap, then reached for the black velvet box. She opened the lid and stared down at the brilliant twinkling of a diamond necklace. Her mouth dropped open and she didn't bother to shut it.

And then you have to go away with him to an island...

This was a nightmare.

And it got worse.

Paul reached back into his breast pocket and pulled out two envelopes emblazoned with a travel agency logo. "Come away with me." He slipped them underneath the velvet box. "Now."

Hillary squeaked and grabbed her water glass, but there wasn't any water, only champagne. And how would that taste when it got to the chocolate crepe stuck in the back of her throat? But of course, champagne went with everything, didn't it?

Especially illicit proposals.

Was this the decision she had to make?

An old-fashioned word came to mind: *mistress*.

Disappointment, surprise and indignation warred within her. She'd been agonizing over life choices and Paul only wanted a fling. Not even a fling among equals. He wanted her to be a... *kept* woman.

At least he remembered she didn't wear fur.

Paul made a small sound.

Hillary hadn't answered him. She hadn't even looked at him.

"I can't stand it." His voice held a suspicious quiver.

Now she looked at him.

He grinned hugely and tears had collected at the outer corners of his eyes. "You should see your face." He bit his lip with the effort of holding back his laughter.

"You beast! You absolute beast! You overheard Natasha babbling on yesterday, didn't you?"

Paul nodded, then gave rein to his laughter.

Hillary felt an annoying mixture of relief and pique. "It would serve you right if I kept this." She dangled the diamond necklace in front of him.

"If you like." Paul's expression told her he was still terribly pleased with himself.

"Fake, right?"

"Not at all. It's a real necklace."

Hillary dumped the sparkling strand back into the box and peeked in the envelopes. They were empty. "I hope you enjoyed your little joke. It ruined the crepe for me."

"I am sorry about that. Do you think you might try to finish it now? I want to talk to you."

He had an earnest expression on his face that didn't help when Hillary tried to swallow. She picked up her fork and wondered if she'd ever be able to eat chocolate again.

"I apologize for the triteness of my small displays of affection."

Hillary felt awful that he'd overheard Natasha. She fervently hoped he hadn't overheard her conversation with Melody. "No, they were lovely."

"But you've been so nervous. Let me explain. When a man gives a woman a single red rose, there is no mistaking his meaning. I didn't have time for you to mistake my meaning. And you haven't, I think."

Hillary put down her fork. "I felt like I was in a paint-by-numbers romance."

Paul sighed. "I thought you would expect a more continental style from me. That perhaps my appeal was as a suave Frenchman."

Hillary, to her extreme annoyance, blushed.

"Some truth to that?" Paul laughed quietly. "I don't mind. It's a part of me. Sometimes I emphasize my European side a little when I'm back here."

"I noticed."

Paul spread his hands. "And it served a purpose with you. I tried to cram six months of Saturday nights into a couple of weeks. I can't take months to date someone."

Perversely, Hillary wondered why she wasn't worth the time... like those other women "friends."

"I've rushed you—I see that now." There was an underlying weariness in Paul's voice. "I had only hoped to—" he hesitated before continuing with a self-deprecating gesture "—engage your affections, as they say, before returning to France."

"Sounds very French."

He made a small sound. "Hillary, I didn't want our relationship to be consumed by a few nights of torrid passion."

Images of sizzling lovemaking bombarded Hillary. But that was all she had—images. All or nothing. He'd been very clever. He was very experienced. It was very frustrating.

"Remember, a slow fire burns hottest."

He was right. Hillary picked at the crepe in silence.

Paul leaned forward. "I have something to ask of you."

All or nothing. Hillary looked up in alarm.

"You must decide—"

"No!" Panic sounded before she could control her voice. "I wasn't expecting..."

A brief smile touched Paul's lips. "Neither was I."

Hillary reached for her champagne and took a large swallow. It fizzed in her nose, making her eyes water. She dabbed at them, disgusted with herself. "In spite of appearances to the contrary, I do have some social polish."

"I know that. Would you believe me if I told you it wouldn't matter?" he asked lightly.

Hillary sniffed. "No."

He responded with a slight shake of his head. "You're probably right, even though these things can be learned." Paul took a deep breath. "All the advance planning for the seminar is completed. I sent the copy of Dominique's perfume off days ago and haven't been bothered by them since. It's time for me to return to France. So...what are we going to do, Hillary?" Paul tugged at his lower lip with his teeth in the way she'd noticed he did before suggesting something he wasn't sure he should. "Come back to France with me."

Hillary stared down at the tablecloth, her hands in her lap. She'd given up all pretense of eating her crepe. She caught a small movement and knew Paul had signaled their waitress to remove her plate.

He was waiting for some sign from her before continuing. "I'm not a tall sultry brunette."

Paul blinked once. "No, you are a petite blond dynamo."

"I am?" Hillary smiled, liking the sound of it, also liking the fact that he'd immediately sensed she needed reassurance.

"Why do you want to be a tall brunette?" Paul steepled his hands and rested them against his lips.

Hillary frowned and toyed with her rose. "I wouldn't look good in St. Etienne clothes."

"Not for another fifty years."

They both smiled. Hillary felt a dangerous rush of affection. Paul was such an intriguing man with his old-world facade and his American upbringing. She could spend a lifetime exploring the different facets of his personality.

Dangerous thoughts. All-or-nothing thoughts.

Paul, the most compelling man she'd ever met, sat across the table from her and offered her something just as enticing as her work.

"I want you to see my home."

Hillary's mind began to whirl. "Now?"

"In a few days. For a visit. You would meet my grandfather."

"Maybe *he'd* like my perfumes," Hillary said aloud, then wished she hadn't.

"He wouldn't like your perfumes, but he would like you," Paul replied. "If he ever got the chance to meet you."

"And I'd love the chance to meet him and prove you wrong about my perfumes." She'd been about to add more when Paul interrupted her, his face beaming.

He leaned forward and squeezed both her hands. "I'll make the arrangements. Do you have a current passport?"

"But Paul, I can't leave now!" A visit was too dangerous. If she went to France now, she'd be lost for sure. After all, he'd have the home-field advantage.

"Why not?"

"Because..." Because her warm heart would overcome her cool head. "Because the Christmas season is just beginning."

"Just for a few days, Hillary. You have Melody and Natasha and her sister to cover for you. They're very capable."

It was true; she could leave if she wanted to. "There would be so many problems if I left right now," she hedged.

"I, too, have problems." He looked deep into her eyes, his voice quietly mesmerizing. "Yet I stole time for you because I recognize that our feelings are rare and precious."

How could she explain that it wasn't the week or so she'd be gone that worried her, but the fear she'd want to stay once she saw St. Etienne? And staying meant giving up everything she'd worked for.

She heard her words of protest even before she'd consciously decided to say them. "I make sixty percent of my yearly income during the Christmas shopping season...."

Paul's face was stony. "Days, Hillary. A few days."

She wasn't handling this at all well. "But France..."

"Yes, France. You could come if you wanted to, but it's fairly obvious I misjudged the depth of your feelings for me."

The words hung between them.

Hillary was miserably aware that she was in a defenseless position. She said nothing.

"Are you going to deny what we feel for each other?"

How was she going to get out of this? "I need more time—"

"How much time?" Paul's angry words interrupted her.

Backed into a corner, Hillary lashed out, "I just don't want to go to France with you now. When I go, I want to go as Hillary Simpson, successful fragrance designer, not a nobody who hasn't made it yet."

A flash of hurt blurred his eyes before he asked with icy calm, "When will you consider yourself successful enough to visit my home?"

"When I have a hit perfume with national distribution."

"Selling your perfumes might take years," Paul pointed out, a heavy sadness hoarsening his voice.

"Not if the seminar is as successful as I think it will be." Hollow comfort, even to her.

Paul caught one of her hands in his. "And if the seminar doesn't lead to a perfume contract?"

"It will," Hillary said with a confidence she wished she felt.

Paul took a slow careful breath and squeezed her hand. "Then you have made your decision."

THE TWENTY-EIGHT ROSES, to which two more could have been added, dominated Scentsations's small display area, making Hillary doubt her decision not to go to France with Paul.

She should have been more candid about her fear of losing herself as his wife, even though he hadn't mentioned marriage. And although Paul didn't consider it important, the Christmas-season sales did take up the slack during non-holiday months when the outrageous mall rent was more than her income.

Maybe she should go to France with him. It was just a trip.... Hillary caught herself, appalled that she was already weakening. She'd be a marshmallow in France.

Paul hadn't come to Scentsations by lunchtime and Hillary felt even worse. Mexican food didn't cheer her up and she didn't dare attempt another chocolate crepe.

There wasn't *anything* that could make her feel better.

Or was there?

Caroline Waite walked through the entrance to Scentsations and Hillary immediately perked up. Had Paul sent her? Was this an "official" visit? Or was Caroline returning for her perfume? Since their parting had been less than cordial, Hillary hadn't mixed a perfume for her.

"Hello, I'm Caroline Waite. We met some weeks ago." Caroline advanced with her hand outstretched.

"Yes, I remember," Hillary replied, as she shook Caroline's hand. "You work for Paul."

Caroline appeared rattled. She looked at Hillary, apparently wanting to say something, but not quite certain how to start.

Hillary felt a bit awkward herself, since she hadn't even begun to mix Caroline's perfume. "I'm glad to see you again," she said, picking up an order pad. "You know, I didn't get your phone number or an address and I had some questions about your scent preferences."

Caroline's beautifully made-up face was blank.

"For your perfume?" Hillary prompted.

"Perfume?"

This was not going well. "You wanted me to compose a perfume for you."

"Oh, that." It seemed to be the opening Caroline needed. She reached into her handbag—a rich brown alligator—and withdrew the samples of Hillary's Sun Shimmers and Moon Shadows. "I quite like these. And so do others," she added with emphasis. "These perfumes are young. They're vibrant. They're America's woman today."

Hillary was afraid to breathe. Had Caroline changed Paul's mind about her perfumes?

"I think your perfumes, Sun Shimmers in particular, would be the perfect fragrance accessory for a line of active, casual clothes for younger women."

"That's what I've been trying to tell Paul!" Hillary said in a rush. "I should have been talking to you all along."

"So you like the idea." Caroline smiled.

"Of course I do!"

"Then you'll like the proposition I have for you even more."

Hillary was about to faint from excitement. "Let's go back to my office where we can talk privately," Hillary offered, hoping that her knees wouldn't give way. She caught her assistant's attention. "I'm not here, Natasha—for anyone."

Paul, you sweet stubborn man, Hillary thought with a rush of affection. Neither one of them would compromise, so he'd sent Caroline. It was better this way. Hillary agreed with Paul; it wasn't wise to do business with friends. Especially if they were going to be more than friends.

Dreaming of a trip to France, she gestured Caroline toward the desk Paul had used and brought an extra chair. "What did you have in mind for my perfumes?"

Hillary listened as Caroline outlined a launch with personal appearances and a series of charity fashion luncheons and shows in upscale department stores, all to begin within a year. The terms were fabulous, surpassing her fantasies, but Hillary had been dreaming of this for a long time and had a few questions.

"If I agree, would I be credited as the perfumer?" She wasn't about to let Maurice St. Etienne steal her glory.

Caroline nodded.

"I want input on the package design and advertising copy."

Caroline nodded again.

Hillary asked for a few minor points, and when these met with immediate approval, she tried for more. "I'd like to be a consultant to the clothes designer." She wouldn't let the staid St. E designers ruin these clothes!

"You have design experience?" Caroline asked with slightly raised eyebrows.

"As a consumer." Hillary smiled. "I simply don't want to be associated with anything frumpy."

Caroline blinked, then her gaze flicked over Hillary.

Hillary knew she looked good. Like Caroline, she wore a black suit, a different cut, but just as sleekly elegant. She wore a cranberry-red charmeuse blouse as acknowledgment of the approaching holiday season. It was a good color for her, a darker version of the natural blush in her cheeks.

"There is no possibility of any of our designs ever being—" Caroline hesitated before speaking the word "—frumpy."

Hillary frowned. Had Caroline ever *seen* St. E clothes?

"Trust me." Caroline sat there with a satisfied, nearly patronizing smile, the kind of smile only someone absolutely sure of her position could give.

Hillary didn't trust her. There was something about that smile, and suddenly Hillary remembered Caroline's comment about being an outsider: *not for long*.

Did Caroline have feelings for Paul? If so, it must be galling to be forced to negotiate with Hillary.

Hillary had better be careful. "I want final approval on the packaging for my perfumes and my name on the box." This was where she found out exactly how committed Paul was to change.

Caroline's eyes narrowed. "You're asking for a lot, aren't you?"

"If these perfumes aren't marketed correctly, they'll bomb. St. Etienne hasn't done a launch like this before and I do have experience."

"But hardly on this scale."

"I want to be involved." Hillary lifted her chin. "I also want a portion of the royalties."

"We'd thought about a lump-sum payment," Caroline countered.

"Maurice St. Etienne receives royalties."

"Yes...but," Caroline shifted uncomfortably and inhaled deeply. "I'm afraid you have the impression that I work for St. Etienne—"

"You said you worked with Paul!" Hillary interrupted in a panic. Was this all a horrible joke?

"At the moment I'm not...with St. Etienne." Caroline cleared her throat. "I represent another fashion and perfume house."

This stunning piece of information rendered Hillary speechless, as Caroline must have known it would.

"I'm sorry the deception was necessary, but I wanted to see if we could come to terms. And we have, I hope."

"But..." But what?

Caroline stood, towering over Hillary. "When I leave, I want you to consider everything we've discussed. I'll be in touch." She picked up her alligator bag and reached inside, extracting a gilt-edged, cream-colored business card.

"Remember, after we launch your perfume, you'll be famous." She handed the card to Hillary.

Engraved across the top was a single word in flowing brown script—*Dominique.*

CHAPTER NINE

"WHAT DO YOU THINK?" Hillary asked as she finished telling Melody about Caroline's offer.

"I think it's quite a coincidence that Dominique would offer to launch your perfumes right now."

"My perfumes are good!"

Melody set a box of single-note fragrances on the glass counter, scattering little bits of brown cardboard over the pristine surface. "What about the perfume you copied? What about their wanting to merge with Paul's company? What about the fact that this Caroline lied to you?"

"I don't know." Hillary slumped onto a black counter stool. "But this is what I've been working toward for years. It was the whole purpose of the seminar."

Melody was silent for a moment. "When do you have to make a decision?"

Hillary swiveled around on the counter stool. "I'm supposed to meet with their lawyers to discuss the contract this afternoon."

"Supposed to?"

Hillary closed her eyes and exhaled. "I feel like a traitor because it's Dominique. It may be my dream, but Caroline has made Paul's life a nightmare."

Melody touched her arm in unspoken sympathy, giving Hillary a comforting pat. "Does he know?"

"Not yet," Hillary answered, staring at the now fully opened roses Paul had given her. "I haven't been able to find him." Just as the words left her lips, Paul himself walked into Scentsations. Melody picked up the box of perfumes, gave Hillary a long look and left the store.

Paul's infamous smile was missing and he seemed low on joie de vivre. "I had an interesting day yesterday," he began conversationally, but with an undertone that warned Hillary all was not well.

"So did I," she countered.

He went on as if she hadn't spoken. "I received a message saying that the Dominique people wanted to meet with me. In Dallas, of all places."

Hillary laughed, more to break the tension than because she was amused. "It's not the end of the world. Just forty-five minutes by plane and most of that is spent circling the airport waiting to land."

Paul didn't laugh. He didn't even smile. "There is also the drive to the airport, the time spent purchasing a ticket, the taxi from the airport to the downtown restaurant, a two-hour wait before I received this..." He dug into his pocket and pulled out a box, pulling off the top to reveal the glass white-rose stopper Hillary had designed for the bottle holding Dominique's perfume copy. Jagged edges of glass spiked the piece of the bottle's neck surrounding the stopper.

"Hey, it worked!" She grinned.

He wasn't amused. "And then there was the whole dreary process in reverse. Someone went to a lot of trouble to ensure my absence."

Caroline. Caroline had wanted Paul out of the way when she made her offer to Hillary. The thought made Hillary feel even guiltier. As her gaze slid away from

Paul's, she noticed Natasha unabashedly eavesdropping. "Let's discuss this in the back."

"So you know something," Paul said, an intimidating expression on his face, the kind that people in positions of power wore so well. It looked especially good on him.

"Perhaps." Hillary drawled the second syllable, hoping for an enigmatic effect. She suspected she wasn't entirely successful. "I had a visit from Caroline Waite."

"She's the Dominique vice president!" Paul was clearly astonished. "But she was to meet me in Dallas!"

Hillary held up a hand. "I didn't know about her connection to Dominique until she handed me her card at the end of our meeting. Before that, I thought she worked for you."

Paul slammed the box with the glass rose onto Hillary's desk. "You'd seen her before and didn't tell me?"

"She asked me not to," Hillary said, trying not to get defensive.

"And you didn't find that strange?"

Hillary sighed. "She acted as if you'd be angry."

"That you were meeting with Dominique's vice president behind my back? Of course I'm angry!"

"I didn't know! When you discussed Dominique, you never referred to their vice president by name. And I thought she'd be French."

"I can't believe this." Paul began to pace. "How did she— Oh, yes. You had your business card sent to her after she interrupted our dinner. What did she want?"

"She was interested in my perfumes—Sun Shimmers and Moon Shadows. In fact, she wants to buy them!"

Hillary blurted. This wasn't the way she had planned to tell him. It sounded too much like "So there!"

Paul stopped pacing and turned to her.

"Well, why not?" she asked, as if he'd spoken. "Dominique has a youthful reputation. Perfect for my perfumes."

"Are you telling me they want to market your perfumes?"

She'd just about had it with this disbelieving tone of his. "They plan to launch them within a year."

Paul sank onto one of Hillary's chairs and stared at the wall. Hillary let him think. "What is she trying to do?" he murmured to himself.

That did it. "Keep her company in step with the times, instead of relying on the moldy aristocracy for support! Targeting real women, not women the way they were fifty years ago."

Paul glanced at her. "Don't be ridiculous. You're an unknown."

His voice was calmly dispassionate, yet Hillary felt as if she'd been slapped. Her knees quivered and she lowered herself onto a convenient, if not entirely sturdy, cardboard box across from him.

"I won't be. By the time I finish making personal appearances and people see my name plastered all over the perfume box—"

"Listen to yourself. They'll never agree to that."

"They already did." She smirked. She'd always wanted to be able to justify a good smirk and this seemed to be the time.

"Have you signed a contract?" Paul shot back.

"Not yet," Hillary admitted, "but I have an appointment this afternoon."

Paul snorted. "Read the fine print."

"Thanks. I will."

Paul continued to stare at her. "Have you any idea what you're getting into?"

He was beginning to sound like Melody. "The time of my life," Hillary replied, raising her chin.

Paul shook his head. "Let me tell you about your new employers—"

"Don't you dare try to spoil this for me! You're just jealous!"

"They're opportunistic sharks. That formula you copied was a gift from my grandfather to the woman he loved. A woman who betrayed him by marrying Gerard Dominique!"

"So why didn't they manufacture the perfume years ago?"

"Do you think Dominique would allow his wife to wear a gift of love from another man?"

Hillary shook her head, even though she didn't know Gerard Dominique.

Paul sat back in the chair. "I doubt Gerard even knew his wife, Chantal, possessed the formula. She died last year. It was presumably with her personal papers."

"I'm sorry," Hillary said automatically, without knowing why.

"Yes." Paul was silent for a moment. "I know my grandfather loved my grandmother but—" he shrugged expressively "—she wasn't Chantal."

"Chantal must have been his first love."

"Yes." Paul nodded. "He's taking her death badly. She was his inspiration. He worked to make St. Etienne a great house, and I think it was to make her regret choosing Gerard. Our houses have always been bitter rivals. Our families are barely cordial to each other."

"So why does Dominique want to merge with St. E?"

"The Dominique family has never been accepted into France's first circles. Most of their sales are foreign. This country, for instance."

"To undiscriminating American women." She made a face.

"Hillary." He spoke quietly, then sighed.

"Paul, it was all so long ago."

"Believe what you wish. The new generation of Dominique executives is ruthless and smart. A dangerous combination. They offered to sell me the formula. I couldn't afford it. They offered to merge with St. Etienne and I can't afford that, either."

Hillary began to nod in understanding. "So they're going to blow you out of the water."

"They'll try." He looked down at his hands briefly, then up at her again. "My grandfather was the only person who ever made me feel wanted. Loved. My own father has forgotten I exist." There was a hard set to Paul's face. "He had the marriage annulled. Annulled. Do you know what that makes me?"

Hillary wasn't sure what to say.

"I interfered with my mother's new life," Paul went on. "I was an annoying reminder of a youthful indiscretion. My grandfather was my family. Is my family. It's my turn to take care of him. I will do anything to protect him and the company he built."

Hillary chose her next words carefully. "I understand—about your loyalty to your grandfather—but Dominique has offered me my dream." She lowered her voice and spoke hesitantly. "It could be our dream.... Now I can come to France...."

The look Paul gave her told her she'd chosen the wrong words. Had his feelings for her changed so quickly?

Anger replaced the hesitancy in her voice. "I had hoped you'd look beyond a rivalry that isn't my concern and be happy for me."

Paul raised his hand, then curled his fingers into a fist, which he dropped onto his knee. "But you know that one day I want it to be your concern. We would share our lives. That means we share our triumphs, our loyalties and our enemies." He punctuated each point by striking his fist against his knee.

"Sure, as long as they're your triumphs, your loyalties and your enemies." The outburst didn't slow her increasing anger. "And while we're at it, how about your name, your country, your business, your family, your style, your clothes—"

Paul grabbed her by the shoulders. "Hillary!"

She squeezed her eyes shut so she wouldn't have to look at him. She'd lost control. She hated losing control.

"Have I *ever* asked those things of you?" he said in an infuriatingly reasonable voice.

Her eyes flew open. "No, you didn't *ask*. You assumed. Isn't that really why you want me to go to France right now? So I can see the mighty St. Etienne and realize how insignificant my wants are?"

He released her, his face whitening.

So she was right. Hillary was surprised at the bitter disappointment she felt. "Congratulations, Paul. It's been an absolutely brilliant campaign. Dazzle the little American and she'll beg for a chance to work for you." She began to clap her hands in slow mocking applause. "Just how far were you willing to go to secure a new perfumer?"

"I thought we meant something to each other," he said quietly.

Hillary noticed how he danced around the word *love*. "So did I."

"Then don't accept the Dominique offer."

"Have you got a better one?" she challenged.

"No." The word, barely audible, was wrenched from him.

Hillary felt guilty, then manipulated. He wanted her to turn down the chance of a lifetime in exchange for some vague hints at a life together.

Maybe she should explain why the Dominique offer was so important to her. "If I sign with Dominique, I'll bring my own identity to... to our life together." Hillary deliberately echoed his words. "That's important to me. And there are advantages. The terms are very generous." She tried a smile that withered at Paul's contemptuous words.

"Do you truly believe Dominique will release perfumes developed by the wife of the head of their greatest rival?"

What an obstinate man he was. "Wife? Did I miss the proposal?"

Paul raked his hand through his hair in the first overt gesture of frustration she'd been able to provoke. "I hadn't planned to... now isn't... but, yes, I hoped that in time... after you saw my home... Damn it, Hillary, I'm the head of a decaying company. I can't give you your dream. You want St. Etienne to launch your perfumes and your ideas. All I have is my heart. Isn't that enough for you?"

He made her sound horrible, like a grasping opportunist who sacrificed love to a career. No, not love. They were avoiding that word.

Pressure began to build behind her temples. Was wanting to sign with Dominique unreasonable? Would she be a pariah at St. Etienne if she did? Should she wait and see what contacts she made at the seminar? Should she go to France? Was she an awful person?

"Paul," Hillary moaned, clutching his shoulders.

He didn't kiss her. She wished he would.

"Forget all of this. Come to France with me," he coaxed gently.

"No!" Hillary jerked back and held her head. "You don't understand!"

"And you have no conception of St. Etienne or you wouldn't refuse to come with me." He spoke sharply, momentarily silencing her. "Your store is smaller than the tiniest St. Etienne boutique. Think big, Hillary. I thought all Texans did."

The bigger they are, the harder they fall. She wanted to say it out loud. Instead, she tried to find a way to make him see the advantages if she signed with Dominique. "I *am* thinking big. And what better revenge than to drain Dominique money into St. Etienne bank accounts?" Hillary felt she had chosen her words very carefully, but Paul nearly exploded with anger.

"No! I forbid you to accept Dominique's offer."

"Forbid. You *forbid?*" Hillary's own anger rose.

But Paul now held himself in icy control. "I'm asking you not to keep your appointment with Dominique. We have no future together if you do."

But the word "forbid" still rang in Hillary's ears. What else would Paul forbid her to do? If she surrendered to him now, he'd expect her to keep surrendering. He'd insist that she fit the mold of a St. Etienne wife— and a St. Etienne perfumer. Hillary Simpson would be no more.

She had to keep the appointment. Hillary stalked to the lab door. "This is my *business*, Paul. It should have nothing to do with our feelings toward each other. Don't ask me to choose one or the other."

She nearly choked at the astonished expression on his face. "I'll let you know what happens. We'll both have had a chance to think things over after my appointment." She picked up the leather envelope she favored over a traditional briefcase and forced herself to leave without looking back at him.

"Hillary, I love you."

Her knees buckled and she gripped the curtained doorway to the lab, ignoring the ominous ripping as strained seams tore.

"That's not fair."

She heard him cross the room. "But it's true." He stood close enough for her to feel his breath warming the back of her neck. If she turned around, she'd be in his arms.

If she turned around, she'd be lost. "Then be happy for me. Wish me good luck."

He murmured something as she made an elegant retreat across the display area of her shop. Only after she reached the parking lot did she realize that he hadn't said good luck. He'd said goodbye.

She was in no condition to meet with Caroline Waite. Hillary started her car and tried to repair her tattered emotions.

Forbid. Paul was as archaic as his company.

If he loved her, shouldn't he be happy for her?

She had made the right choice. The only choice. She'd be swallowed up at St. Etienne. There would be no more Hillary Simpson. Her only identity would be as Paul's wife.

She repeated the litany over and over during the drive, not looking at her watch until she was in front of the elevators in the sleek, glass high-rise housing Dominique's lawyers. The office building was new and contemporary, just like Dominique. Just like Sun Shimmers and Moon Shadows.

She was relatively calm as she searched the building directory for a snack bar or lounge in which to spend the hour she had to wait. Paul was being unreasonable and by now he must surely realize it, Hillary thought as she punched the elevator button for the basement. She was going to be a very rich woman. So what if her money came from Dominique?

Paul was very hardheaded. When he was less angry and he could think about Hillary's working for Dominique less emotionally, he ought to see poetic justice in Dominique's making a St. Etienne wife, assuming Hillary agreed to be a St. Etienne wife, famous. Then Dominique's own money would help fight off the merger attempt. It was beautifully clever and a much more subtle form of revenge than butting heads with Caroline Waite, which was what Paul had been doing up to now.

Paul. He'd been struggling and fighting to keep his company together for so long—and from what he'd said, without his family's help—that he was unable to step back and try a different way.

Paul. He'd said he loved her. Did she...? She couldn't think about that now. She had enough to think about. He had no right to bring love up like... a trump card.

Hillary took a deep breath, clearly seeing what she had to do. She had to sign with Dominique. Paul might be angry for a while, but he'd soon realize that when Dominique launched her perfumes, Hillary could have her dreams and he could save St. Etienne.

The elevator opened into a small basement lounge, occupied by a lone man. Hillary faced the row of vending machines, her stomach rebelling at the sight of plastic-encased food. She bought a soft drink and turned away from the machines, aware that she was alone in the basement with a strange man. No one else had entered the snack area.

Hillary hesitated, wondering whether to stay and sip her drink, or leave. Although the man appeared engrossed in his magazine, she edged toward the elevators. She glanced at the man once more, then saw the cover of the magazine he was reading. *Perfumer's Quarterly.* He must be Dominique's perfumer, she thought, and had arrived early for the meeting, too.

Wearing a professionally pleasant smile, she approached him. He was youngish but had gone soft, with a receding hairline and black-framed glasses. "Excuse me, are you the consulting perfumer for Dominique?"

"One of them," he answered and rose to his feet.

Hillary extended her hand. "I'm Hillary Simpson."

"Alain Brun," he responded with a slight but unmistakable French accent. "I suppose this is not common reading material." He closed the magazine.

"We're both early."

"Yes. I have heard many horror stories of Houston traffic and was told to allow plenty of time."

"It's all the road construction." They were still standing, and Hillary realized they would remain that way until she sat down. She did so, taking two deep breaths and reminding herself not to gush.

Alain Brun must have noticed her nervousness. "Do not worry. I am only here to make certain you do not present us with a formula for, say, ketchup, or floor cleaner, or..."

Hillary cautiously relaxed the hold on her tongue. "This is the first time I've sold my formulas, and everything has happened so quickly. Caroline says they'll launch these within a year. It's rather exciting. I'm going to help design the box and the bottle, then I'll tour—'' Hillary stopped for breath.

Alain's gaze dropped to his hands. If Hillary hadn't been so intensely aware of his reactions, she wouldn't have thought anything of it.

Suddenly, she realized the awkward position Alain must be in. *He* had probably never had the credit she was going to get.

How insensitive of her. She changed the subject.

''Have you heard about my seminar? It was announced in the spring issue of *Perfumer's Quarterly,* but I had to postpone it.'' She was babbling again. She slowed her speech. ''Anyway, it's planned for this spring. Would you like to come? A St. Etienne representative will be there.''

As she spoke, Hillary realized she was talking about Dominique's greatest rival.

''Maybe I won't be able to handle the seminar if Dominique needs me then...'' Hillary trailed off, conscious that she'd managed to insult Alain on several fronts. First the wonderful terms of her contract, then touting a seminar featuring his rival, then practically rescinding her seminar invitation because she might be too busy promoting perfumes *he* still had to endorse. It would serve her right if he recommended that she donate her perfumes to handicapped skunks.

Alain smiled tightly. ''I would carry on with the seminar. It sounds intriguing.''

''But if Dominique starts production, they'll need my input.''

"All I have to do is mix one bottle and they are in production. And, of course, I will do that immediately in order to begin market tests with the fragrance."

"*One* bottle? But I'm supposed to make appearances... The launch... I'm to help design the packaging..."

Alain gave her a look very much like the ones Melody, and now Paul, regularly gave her. "You are very young and very eager." Why did all men see her that way? "I... know the schedule somewhat and I doubt very much if there will be the kind of launch you are expecting within that amount of time."

"But the contract..." Surely Alain was mistaken.

He shrugged in a very French way.

The gesture reminded her of Paul and sent a pang through her. Was he still angry? She wished he was there with her. He'd see through any legal shenanigans.

"But your solicitor will see to all that."

"Mmm, yes." She hadn't even mentioned the offer to her lawyer.

Hillary realized that she'd been very foolish. Paul had tried to warn her, but she'd been so intent on becoming famous and saving St. Etienne, she hadn't listened. And now that she was able to think rationally, why would Caroline plan a launch that would compete with the perfume created by Paul's grandfather? The more Hillary thought about it, the more uneasy she became. Everything had seemed so clear moments ago. Now what should she do?

"It is time we went to the meeting." Alain smiled at her, tactfully not mentioning the disillusionment he must have known she felt.

Hillary decided she wouldn't sign until she had the contract examined by her lawyer. And Paul. She should have remembered that when something sounded too good to be true, it usually was. How had Paul stood her smugness? She was in for a good dose of I-told-you-so's.

An extremely confident Caroline greeted her. "Here's your contract, Hillary. If you look it over, you'll find that it's along the lines of our verbal agreement."

The contract was much more complicated than Hillary had expected. The Dominique lawyers probably used a lot of words to hide their tricky loopholes.

"Now, if Alain could see the formulas?"

Hillary was nervous as she withdrew the papers. This was the first time she'd ever shown another perfumer her mixtures.

She glanced at the contract while Alain studied her formulas. His face was expressionless, except for the occasional raised eyebrow.

The minutes ticked by. Hillary found clauses informing her that production and marketing were entirely separate. If it hadn't been for Alain, she wouldn't have thought anything was unusual. Now she was suspicious of everything.

"I see I am due for some competition," he remarked at last. "Interesting. I have recently noted the trend toward more natural ingredients."

Hillary's nerves were soothed by the compliment. She'd rarely had the opportunity to talk with a colleague. "I wanted to work with the changes that time and sunlight would make on the perfumes. I used oils that didn't break down as quickly."

Alain nodded and returned the papers to her. "I look forward to sampling these. You are very talented."

Alain was generous to disregard her earlier thoughtlessness and to compliment her, as well. Relief washed over her. She knew she had talent, but it was nice to have someone else recognize it.

Suddenly Hillary experienced an intense longing for Paul. They should be negotiating this together. It affected both their futures; it was only right that he be there.

Both their futures. Hillary caught her breath as she realized what her thoughts meant. Her future was with Paul, because she was in love with Paul.

Of course she was in love with him and had been for a long time. How silly not to realize it before. It was a relief, sheer relief to acknowledge her feelings, as Paul had acknowledged his. Tension drained from her. She didn't need to fight falling in love. There was nothing to fear. With love, she and Paul could work everything out. All the harsh words they'd spoken could have remained unsaid. He was going to be so proud of her.

Elated, Hillary could hardly wait for the meeting to end so that she could race back to Paul's hotel. She would admit that she loved him and they'd fall into each other's arms. Then they'd discuss the Dominique contract—after a certain amount of time spent making up.

She smiled at the thought, then found her smile answered by Caroline. "Well, Hillary, if you're ready," Caroline handed her a gold pen.

"I'd like my lawyer to take a look at this first," Hillary said.

"Fine," Caroline replied smoothly. "Will your lawyer be here soon?"

"I'll take the contract to her." Hillary reached for her case.

A frown marred the cosmetic perfection of Caroline's face. "Hillary, we want to do this today. You should have made arrangements before now. We need an answer.''

"I'm sorry." Caroline was right and Hillary had committed a terrible business faux pas. "I had no idea the contract would be so lengthy and complicated."

"The only thing you need to understand is the amount right here." Caroline pointed to the payment Hillary would receive upon signing.

"There are some other points I'd like clarified." Hillary was purposely vague. "Time frames and so on."

"Such as?"

"I . . ." Her eyes met Alain's, which were carefully neutral. Hillary assumed that Caroline was aware of her association with Paul, so Alain wouldn't be censured for divulging company secrets. "I've heard you're planning another perfume launch. I don't see how you could launch my perfumes next year, too." Hillary flipped through the pages of the contract. "In fact, there isn't anything in here detailing the type of launch and personal appearances we discussed."

"That would be difficult to put in a contract."

Hillary gave Caroline a level look. "I'd like my lawyer to try." She slid the gold pen back across the table.

Caroline stared at it. "I'm going to have to insist you make a decision now, with the contract as it is. You do realize that you can walk out of here with a check for one hundred thousand dollars?"

It was a lot of money, but she'd make millions when her perfumes were marketed. "Why are you in such a hurry?"

Alain spoke. "So you won't sell your perfumes to someone else."

Caroline turned to her consultant, the look of tight-lipped fury on her face clearly warning him to keep quiet.

She was too late. Hillary finally understood. "It's Paul. You're buying my perfumes because you don't want Paul to have them," she said slowly, feeling her happiness evaporate.

"Hillary," Caroline began placatingly, "the reason we're buying them shouldn't be important to you. The fact is we do want to buy them."

Hillary felt sick. The reason was terribly important to her. They didn't want her perfumes. They wanted to thwart Paul. How could they know that St. Etienne had no intention of producing her perfumes?

And neither did Dominique. Caroline saw Hillary as a threat to the merger and was taking steps to eliminate that threat.

Disillusionment was a heavy weight in her chest, making it difficult for her to stand, but she struggled to her feet, anyway. "If I sell them to you, that's the last I see of them, right?"

"Not necessarily."

Hillary shook her head. "Nice try, Caroline."

"Wait." The imperiously spoken word stopped her. "We'll double any offer St. Etienne has made."

Two husbands? The thought made Hillary laugh, which angered Caroline. She cut off Hillary's explanation. "You should reconsider." Caroline tapped the gold pen. "St. Etienne won't last another year."

"Oh, I don't know," Hillary said. "Paul still has a plan or two."

"Surely you aren't referring to your little seminar."

She was, but for once in her life, Hillary held her tongue. If Caroline didn't know that St. Etienne needed a new perfumer, she wouldn't learn it from Hillary.

Hillary left shortly afterward, conscious that she had made an enemy. She sat in her car until she stopped shaking. What a fool. If only she'd listened. If only Paul had tried to understand.

She drove directly to his hotel. She and Paul could work out their relationship. They had to. And then Hillary was going to help him save St. Etienne from Caroline.

Caroline had lied to her, insulted her and belittled her. Caroline was a threat to the man Hillary loved.

She anxiously rode the elevator to his suite and hurried down the carpeted hall.

The door stood open as a maid vacuumed. Hillary's gaze shot toward the bedroom and took in the empty suitcase stand and the bundle of sheets stripped from the bed.

Paul St. Steven was gone.

CHAPTER TEN

PAUL WAS GONE. The hotel clerk confirmed what Hillary already knew. She waited for the crushing wave of grief, but felt only a shaky emptiness.

She refused to believe that Paul had left. He couldn't be gone. He wouldn't leave after telling her he loved her, would he? They were both quick-tempered. Hillary remembered his impulsive visit to the Renaissance Festival. He probably already regretted checking out of the hotel and would call her soon or come by Scentsations. She'd better return to the store.

Hillary paused at the Scentsations entrance, breathing deeply and waiting for the familiar rush of pride. She'd worked hard to build Scentsations, spending long hours in her lab after the shop closed. The perfume she'd designed for Toodle Lou's was selling well, resulting in a commission from a lingerie shop. So, in spite of the Dominique fiasco, she knew she had talent. Paul didn't expect her to turn her back on all this, did he?

As she gazed into her shop, the amber perfumes didn't seem so rich anymore. The cut glass had lost its sparkle, and as she stepped inside, the whole shop seemed stuffy and hot. She dimmed the lights.

Natasha looked up from her incessant counter-spritzing. "Paul left this for you." For once subdued, she handed Hillary an envelope bearing the name of Paul's hotel and went back to obliterating fingerprints.

Apprehension shivered through her. "Thanks." Hillary managed a perfunctory smile for Natasha's benefit, but Natasha wasn't looking at her.

The envelope contained a check wrapped in a single sheet of hotel stationery. "For the perfume copy. If the amount is insufficient, please bill me for the difference. Goodbye."

She noticed Paul had used "goodbye" and not "au revoir." "Goodbye" was final. "Au revoir" meant he'd see her again. As she stared at the scrawled words, Hillary's heart began to pound. He'd been furious and hurt when he'd written this, far more hurt than furious. Anger cooled quickly. Wounds took much longer to heal. She'd been hurting, too, but Paul had been vulnerable. He'd told her he loved her, and she'd gone to Dominique, anyway.

Hillary bowed her head over the terse note as she realized the magnitude of her actions. She'd lost Paul, and it hurt far more than knowing Caroline, of Dominique, had lied to her.

"He's going back to France, isn't he?" Natasha asked.

"It appears that way." But she didn't know, did she? Had Paul spoken with Natasha? Hillary swallowed her pride. "Did . . . did he tell you his plans?"

The spray bottle hissed and Natasha's soft cloth squeaked over the glass display. "No, but he did hang around talking to me. Asked me what I wanted to do with my life. Said he liked my style. He told me I ought to go on to school, but I've had enough of studying."

Hillary drank in Natasha's words, imagining the conversation. Paul had recovered from the first heat of anger if he had spent time with Natasha. This was no impulsive flight home. Hillary's hands were cold and her stomach churned. It didn't sound as if Paul was going to change his mind on the drive to the airport.

"Melody was here, too. Her frankincense and myrrh order came in."

"Did they talk?"

"Not about you."

"What *did* they talk about?" Hillary's voice had an edge to it. She hated pumping Natasha for information.

"He told Melody not to make the same mistake he had." Natasha stopped wiping the counter and wrinkled her forehead. "He said that sometimes you have to change in order to keep things the same. What does that mean?"

Hillary exhaled in a loud whoosh. "It means he should have waited and talked to me instead of you and Melody."

"I figure your fight isn't any of my business, but it must have been a humdinger."

"We didn't fight," Hillary said slowly. "We each felt very strongly about something and neither of us chose to compromise."

But *she* had offered a compromise, Hillary thought. Paul had been unfair in issuing his ultimatum. Hillary would have discussed her meeting with him had he bothered to wait.

She squared her shoulders. He had talked with Natasha and Melody, but he hadn't talked with her. A few minutes earlier, she would have crawled to France and groveled once she got there. But not now.

Hillary walked back to the lab and sat at her desk, tapping the envelope against the surface. Looking at the check, she saw the amount was more than enough to cover the perfume copy she had mixed for Paul. What a mess. She covered her face with her hands and tried to sort out the tangle.

She was in love with a man who apparently espoused another generation's attitudes toward women. How fortunate that she'd discovered it now, she told herself, before she got hurt.

Hillary swallowed. She didn't feel fortunate. She felt cheated. A few hours ago, she'd had everything. Now she had nothing.

Hillary dropped her hands into her lap. The seminar. The seminar was the key to everything. It would be her only link to Paul; not only that, it would be a way to help him fight Dominique's merger attempt.

He needed the publicity his perfumer's grant would bring. Hillary needed the contacts. And they each needed an excuse to remain in touch without losing face.

Hillary drew a piece of writing paper toward her. She'd send Paul a note and a check for the difference between her invoice and the money he'd left.

What to write? No accusations. No why-did-you-leave's. No pleading. She would inform him that she intended to proceed with the seminar as they had planned. Paul was a proud man, but not a foolish one. The seminar would benefit him, as well as her.

"Decided not to go with Dominique," she wrote. "Now I can concentrate on our seminar. I'm determined that it will be a fabulous success for both of us. Regards to your grandfather." She purposely left only enough room at the bottom of the page to sign her name.

Hillary read the note, pleased that it was warmly cordial, yet wouldn't embarrass Paul if his secretary opened it. He'd be able to tell that she wasn't holding a grudge. The tantalizing bit of information about not selling to Dominique should prompt a phone call.

And Hillary would be ready for that call.

It didn't come.

What did come, nearly hidden in the Christmas mail, was a note, matching the tepid tone of hers. "Dear Hillary," it began. Not *my dear,* or *dearest,* but plain *dear.* "You made a quick decision re: Dominique. I find I need more time—time without pressure. Best of luck with your seminar. I'll contact you when I've made a decision. Regards, Paul."

In other words, don't call me, I'll call you.

Hillary blinked back tears as her mind repeated key words: he needed time... *your* seminar... no pressure... *I'll* contact you. So. It appeared that not only had Hillary lost Paul personally, she might have lost him for the seminar, too.

Okay, he wanted time, she'd give him time. But the seminar would be so fantastic, he'd *have* to come back for it.

Christmas was in five days. Hillary had an up-to-date passport and two airline reservations—one to New York, where she could take the train to her parents' home for Christmas, and one continuing from New York to Paris, where she could meet Paul for Christmas. Dry-eyed, Hillary picked up the phone, called her travel agent and canceled her ticket to Paris.

"WHAT ARE YOU DOING to the window?" Melody squeezed her lotions and soaps closer together, making room on the shelves for bath oils.

"Trying to lure the college students back into the store," Hillary replied from the display window where she tacked up red satin. "They disappeared after doing all their Christmas shopping." She didn't look back at Melody, knowing she would see tight-lipped disapproval. Red satin didn't really go with Earth Scents. But red satin did go with Valentine's Day and she hoped to boost Melody's sales. Melody had too many products crowding the shelves.

"Love oils from literature?" Melody read from a hand-lettered card by the staple gun. "Who's going to be attracted by that?"

"It's worth a try." Hillary risked a glance down at Melody. "Retailers commonly tie in to the holidays."

"What do you plan for Saint Patrick's Day? Leprechaun Lotion?"

"Sure, why not? Celery hasn't been moving too well lately, has it?"

"Who can find it?" Melody frowned. "The shop is so cluttered . . . so crowded. The atmosphere isn't peaceful anymore. My customers' souls are assaulted."

"You don't have that many customers."

"I have plenty of customers!"

"You have plenty of browsers." Melody kept a pot of herb tea on all day and many who came into Earth Scents sampled tea and purchased nothing.

Hillary squatted on the windowsill and tacked lace around the edge. "That's why the mail-order business will be perfect for you."

Melody went very still. "What mail-order business?"

Hillary closed her eyes. Drat Ben! Hadn't he told Melody yet? "Ben and I kind of kicked the idea around. Think about it. You could keep the front open here and have tea and chat with your friends. The rest of the time, you could fill orders." Hillary stood, smiling. "How does that sound?"

"Like a lot of work."

Hillary turned around so that Melody wouldn't see the disappointed expression on her face. As sales traffic decreased, Melody had become accustomed to the quiet, serene days at Earth Scents. She drank her tea, did light—very light—bookkeeping and stared out the windows of her shop. Hillary had spent entire mornings there when not even one person had come in. Melody was very dear to her, a calming influence on her own impetuosity. However...

"Mail order would take more effort, but your kids are old enough to help...a lot of the work is already done."

"What do you mean?" Suspicion shaded Melody's voice.

"First, you need a catalog—"

"The photographer! I thought he was photographing for your seminar brochures!"

Hillary nodded. "He did that, too."

"You arranged everything without telling me?"

Hillary expected to hear relief. There was only anger. "I wanted it to be a surprise."

"No," Melody said in what was for her a firm voice. "You wanted me to go along with your ideas without making any fuss."

"We didn't want to upset you."

"I am upset!" Melody sat down, her agitation evident.

Everything had gone wrong. "Please, Melody. I tried to find a way to increase your sales *without* upsetting you."

"You'd better stop worrying about *my* sales and start worrying about *your* seminar! When are you going to get in touch with Paul?"

Hillary reeled from Melody's unexpected attack. Gentle Melody had hit a low blow. Hillary ran a shaky hand through her hair. Melody had been her rock these past few weeks, just as she had always been. Hillary couldn't have endured the Christmas season and finalized seminar details without Melody's support. The mail-order idea had seemed like a way to repay Melody, but it had only angered her.

"Paul wanted time. He said he'd contact me."

"You haven't heard from him since that note. You can't keep making seminar plans that involve him without telling him about them."

Hillary's eyes began to sting. She couldn't think about Paul. She had immersed herself in work trying to forget her feelings for him as he had apparently forgotten his feelings for her. Over and over she asked herself how he could declare his love one minute and walk out of her life the next.

"He's still coming, isn't he?"

Hillary closed her eyes.

"Oh, Hillary." The gentle Melody had returned.

Hillary squeezed back her tears and jumped down from the display window. "I haven't heard that he isn't."

"But you've been telling everyone he's coming! My storeroom is filled with seminar literature. What will you do if he doesn't show up?"

A package delivery van rumbled down the street outside Earth Scents, interrupting Hillary's reply, which was just as well. She and Melody were about to quarrel again.

The squealing brakes and two beeps from the horn announced that the van had stopped. "I'll answer that," Hillary said, hurrying toward the back.

"There's more?" Melody called, accusation ringing in her voice. "There isn't any room!"

"You have more space here than I've got left at Scentsations or my apartment." Hillary signed the receipt and handed the clipboard back to the driver. "We can move your desk out front."

"I don't want my desk out front!" Melody had followed her.

"It'll just be a little while."

"Is all that for us? Where will we put my supplies?"

"The boxes will stack," Hillary tried to reassure her partner as box after box was wheeled out of the van. It *did* look like a lot.

"Don't think we can stack these more than three high, ma'am," said the driver. "Too heavy."

"Uh," Hillary looked around, avoiding Melody's eyes. "We'll make an aisle, then."

Melody was silent until the delivery van pulled away. "How much did this cost?" she asked from behind a brown column.

Hillary began slitting open boxes. "You get what you pay for. This is going to be a first-class seminar. Glossy paper, elegant printing—"

"How many copies did you order?"

Hillary looked up from the seminar brochure she was proofreading and sighed. "Ten thousand. You get a price break—"

"Hillary!" Melody held a hand to her temple. "I can't stand it anymore! You aren't going to have ten thousand people at your seminar!"

"Calm down and listen to me. These will be inserts in *Perfumer's Quarterly*. People will use them to register. I didn't order so much of anything else."

"How are we supposed to work in here?" Melody asked as Hillary opened another box.

"I'll ship the inserts off to the magazine this week."

"What are those?" Melody pointed to a slick glossy magazine.

"Your catalogs. Aren't they gorgeous?"

Melody picked one up. "And how much did they cost?"

"A lot," Hillary admitted without giving any details. "You need a catalog to run a mail-order business."

Melody's hand crept back to her temple. "I didn't know we had a mail-order business."

Hillary counted to three before replying. "Ben and I think it has great potential."

"I didn't agree to anything!"

"It's a good idea, isn't it?"

"Yes," Melody conceded, "but not immediately." She tossed the catalog back into the box.

"Of course not immediately. After the seminar." It was obvious that Melody needed some time to get used to the idea.

Melody closed her eyes, both hands now massaging her temples. "Why didn't you consult me?"

Hillary was puzzled. "Because I always handle the details. You never want to." What was happening to Melody? She'd never acted like this. The one person Hillary could count on to remain consistent, unchanging, was Melody.

Melody didn't open her eyes. "This is more than a detail." Her voice quivered.

"I'm sorry." Hillary found herself offering comfort to Melody. It felt strange. "Forget about the mail-order business." Why hadn't Ben warned her that he was keeping everything from his wife? "I made a mistake."

"You can't send the catalogs back."

"Don't worry, Melody. Please."

"And all of this!" Melody opened her eyes and waved her arms at the boxes filling the storeroom. "You are obsessed with making this seminar perfect. You think it's going to solve all your problems."

Hillary tilted her chin. "It could."

Melody moved a box so that she could sit down. In the process, she found the packing list and opened the seal before Hillary could stop her.

Melody gasped.

"Keep in mind that this is an expense the seminar fee is supposed to cover," Hillary said.

"Don't patronize me!" Melody spoke sharply, one of the rare times Hillary had heard her do so. "Hundreds of people would have to register for you to break even. And you don't even know if your big draw is still planning to come, do you?"

Hillary felt like a little girl being chastised. "No."

Melody's deep breaths caught in a sob. "Look at this." She thrust a brochure in Hillary's face. "St. Etienne's name is on here more than yours and they haven't paid any of the expenses." She gestured toward the packing slip. "That's just one bill and the total is almost as much as we have in savings. No wonder you wanted to increase my store traffic!"

"Melody!" Hillary wailed her name. No seminar was worth upsetting her friend like this.

"How could you spend so much money?" Melody began to rock from side to side, her lips moving in a silent chant.

Hillary touched her arm. "Melody?"

There was no response, just a determined chanting.

What was wrong? Hillary had taken financial risks before. Why was Melody so upset now? "It'll be okay. I'll pay for everything myself."

"I'm here, Melody." Ben stood in the doorway lead-
ing to the apartment over the shop, a stern expression on
his face. "Go on upstairs and have some tea. The water's ready." He reached out to guide his wife up the
steps. Melody stumbled and clung to him. He turned
toward Hillary, with a weary smile, his eyes sad. "We
have to talk."

STRESS. HOW COULD serene Melody suffer from stress?
And how could Hillary have missed the signs?

All the years she had thought she was taking care of
Melody, Melody had thought she was taking care of her.
It had been an unusual partnership, and now, with a
resolution to dissolve and a statement that their taxes
were paid, their legal ties were officially severed. Hillary found it difficult to believe that it took only days to
end what she and Melody had spent years building. She
was left with a hollow feeling and wondered if divorce
affected people the same way.

Melody and her family were moving to the site of the
Renaissance Festival, where they would live—and run
their mail-order business. Once Ben explained that the
mail-order business would make the move possible,
Melody was profoundly grateful to Hillary. The Ander-
sons were looking forward to their move. Hillary wasn't.

All she had left was the seminar. The seminar was her
chance for happiness. It was her chance for success and
her chance to get Paul back.

Hillary sat in the storeroom opening and resealing the
boxes of seminar brochures. She wanted no possibility
of a mistake this time, otherwise she would have had
them shipped directly to the magazine.

The brochures were richly elegant and understated.
She hoped Paul approved. Hillary admired the raised

foil lettering linking the Scentsations and St. Etienne names. It was worth every penny.

The delivery van beeped its horn and soon the brochures were loaded and on their way.

Hillary rearranged the storeroom and dragged the desk back inside. She had one more chore. One box, smaller than the rest, contained formal invitations to the seminar. She planned to mail those to selected individuals herself.

And the first one was going to St. Etienne.

That should provoke a reaction. Paul, with his impeccable manners, would never ignore an RSVP.

Over the next few weeks, Hillary regularly felt sorry for herself, a feeling she realized was completely selfish. The thought of Melody's moving away always prompted a bout of self-pity. Hillary didn't find this to be an especially attractive feature in herself and so put on a cheery mask, which she realized fooled no one, but made her feel better.

"Shall I leave some of the Leprechaun Lotion?" Melody asked as she happily packed her boxes. Ben and the children had already driven the rental truck with their household furnishings to the Elizabethan duplex that would be their new home and shop. Other families who felt the same way about city life lived at the Renaissance Festival site, too. For now, Earth Scents would become their mail-order warehouse, so it wasn't as if Hillary would never see Melody again. In fact, Melody's two children were finishing the school year in Houston.

"Leprechaun Lotion?" Hillary thought for a minute. "Yes, but I doubt I'll sell much."

Melody nodded. "Right. Let's see…I'll trade you for some of your pretty bottles."

Hillary gave her a wide smile. Melody was learning. She'd do just fine. "They're stored in the back."

While Melody selected her bottles, Hillary untied the bunches of dried flowers that hung from the ceiling. Melody would be taking those with her to decorate their festival cottage.

"Hillary, Ben brought your seminar mail over from Scentsations." Melody appeared at the bottom of the ladder and set a pile of envelopes on an empty shelf next to it. "Don't forget to save the stamps. The kids love them."

"Okay."

Melody tapped the pile. "Your mail's right here, then."

Hillary nodded. "I'll look at it in a minute." She carefully detached the string from the crumbling flowers.

Melody hesitated. "Don't forget."

Hillary looked down at her. *"Okay."* What was that all about? she wondered, watching Melody saunter off. She scrambled down from the ladder. Melody had left the heavy cream envelope from St. Etienne on top.

Hillary ripped it open, conscious that she should be using a sterling-silver letter knife. It was that kind of paper.

My dear Hillary,
There is much for us to discuss, but it will have to wait until I can see you. Now I can only tell you that, under the circumstances, it will be impossible for me to represent St. Etienne at the seminar. I'm sure you agree.

Warmest regards, Paul

"No!"

"What?" Melody had not gone far.

Hillary couldn't answer. She could barely think. "No!" she cried again.

Melody tugged the letter from Hillary's shaking fingers.

How could he do that to her? How could he back out at the last minute? How could he humiliate her in front of the entire perfume industry? Last year's embarrassment was nothing compared to this disaster. Hillary began walking toward the storeroom, ignoring Melody's faint exclamation.

Warmest regards. Hillary went directly to the telephone and began punching in a number she had memorized long ago—the country code, everything. *I'm sure you agree.* Ha!

Relays clicked and a French voice spoke. Hillary responded in English. She wasn't about to try her rusty French again.

"Paul St. Steven." She wouldn't even say the St. Etienne name.

More French.

Hillary repeated Paul's name and obstinately continued to do so until another heavily accented voice came on the line.

"I regret that Monsieur St. Etienne is not accepting any telephone calls at this time."

"Tell him it's Hillary Simpson."

The voice repeated its message.

"Tell him!"

Silence and then another voice, female, and with much less of an accent.

"I am Jeanette Poulenc, Monsieur St. Etienne's assistant. He is unavailable."

"Then get him!" Hillary wasn't trying for an award in diplomacy.

"It is evening here, almost everyone is at home."

The time difference. Hillary felt stupid.

"Are you with the press?" the woman asked.

"No," Hillary stated in a much calmer voice.

With skillfully soothing questions, Paul's assistant was able to persuade Hillary to explain about the seminar.

"I will look at his calendar."

Hillary heard pages flip. "I am so very sorry, but Monsieur St. Etienne will not be returning before that time."

"Where is he?" Hillary demanded.

"He is out of the country."

"Well, is he in *my* country?"

Hillary heard the woman breathe deeply before replying, "I do not know where Monsieur St. Etienne is at this precise moment."

And you wouldn't tell me if you did.

"I will leave him a message—"

"Never mind," Hillary interrupted wearily. "I've tried that before." Trying to salvage something of Franco-American relations, Hillary thanked Paul's assistant and hung up the phone. She then reached into the nearest box of seminar literature and began ripping forms into small pieces.

Melody grabbed her arm. "Stop it!"

"Why?" Hillary snatched her arm back and ripped another registration form. "This is all useless. A huge waste of money. In fact, as you pointed out, I can't afford to have the literature reprinted."

"You can salvage this. You *always* think of something."

"Not this time." Hillary picked up one of the shock-ingly expensive, embossed leatherette binders each reg-istrant would have received and threw it against the wall.

"Hey!"

Hillary abandoned the binders and reached for the registration acknowledgments. They were of such good quality paper that they were difficult to tear.

"This is a better tantrum than either of my children ever threw," Melody said. Hillary crossed her arms over her chest. "You're better at pouting, too."

A tear slid down Hillary's cheek. She knew it was the first of many. "I am going to be the joke of the indus-try. A *broke* joke."

"Only if you let yourself be."

"Oh, come on, Melody! What else will people think after I cancel a seminar two years in a row?"

"You aren't going to cancel the seminar," Melody said briskly.

Hillary looked at her in disbelief.

"His note says, 'under the circumstances.' That's a nice elastic phrase you can stretch to fit your needs when you explain Paul's absence."

"Melody," Hillary said smiling through her tears, "I didn't know you practiced the finer art of deception."

Melody blushed. "Something else—you can accept applications for the St. Etienne perfume grant and box them up and ship them off after the seminar. In fact, videotape interviews and include them," she finished triumphantly.

Hillary grinned and grabbed a tissue from the box on the desk. "It figures. Just when I get you good and trained, you leave."

"I want to help you with this seminar, Hillary. I'm so happy living away from Houston. You made it possible. I'll be driving the kids to school each day and I can help you then."

"Thanks, Melody, but you know this seminar was as much for Paul as it was for me." Hillary grabbed another tissue as she felt tears welling up. "How can I go on without him?"

"You just will."

The arrival of a second cream envelope from St. Etienne the following day triggered Hillary's anguish, rage and frustration all over again. This time she was at Scentsations and quickly hurried back into the lab. Melody was right behind her.

Hillary drew a deep breath, then tore open the envelope.

Maurice St. Etienne accepts with pleasure the kind invitation...

Maurice?

"It says *Maurice* St. Etienne is coming to the seminar."

Melody peered over Hillary's shoulder. "Maurice? Are you sure?"

"That's what it says." Hillary was now reading the note for the fourth time.

Melody pressed both hands against her mouth. "This is fantastic! We've got to let people know. Hillary! Call the hotel and have them hold more rooms in the block. You've got to play this up."

"Uh..."

Melody laughed. "Look at you! You're so shocked you can't think." Melody began to sort through the rest of the stack of envelopes. "You know, you ought to plan a reception or something to honor Maurice. That would give you an excuse to send out another round of invitations without looking like you were desperate for people to come.''

Hillary sat on one of the ubiquitous brown boxes.

''Hey.'' Melody touched her shoulder. ''What's wrong?''

''I thought Paul might change his mind, but he's still not coming. Now he's sending his grandfather.'' Hillary's throat tightened. She saw the sympathy in Melody's eyes and quickly looked away.

''I guess he really doesn't want to see me again,'' she choked out.

''Are you giving up?'' The sympathy was gone. Melody actually sounded angry.

''What more can I do?''

''Figure out how you can make the most of Maurice's presence at your seminar.'' Melody hesitated before continuing. ''Then fly to France immediately after it's over and show Paul what pressure really is.''

With both Melody and Natasha treating her as though they expected her to fall apart, burst into tears or begin throwing things, Hillary rallied, splurging on engraved invitations to a reception honoring Maurice St. Etienne. She decided she'd send one to Paul, then ruined two envelopes writing the address.

Two weeks before the seminar, Hillary worked her way through a small mountain of mail, freezing as she came to another heavy cream envelope, sealed with gold wax impressed with a rose. A familiar sweet fragrance clung to it, intensifying when Hillary broke the seal.

It was an announcement. Hillary stopped breathing as she scanned the text.

The French Houses of Dominique and St. Etienne
are pleased to announce their merger, which they
are celebrating with the release of a magnificent new
perfume created by the legendary Maurice St.
Etienne. Please present this card at the fragrance
counter in better department stores for your com-
plimentary sample of Chantal.

Hillary brought the card to her nose and inhaled, releasing a flood of memories and a flood of tears.

CHAPTER ELEVEN

"YOU'RE RIGHT. Everyone did wear black." Melody, her long hair wrapped in a gold net snood, eyed Hillary, who wore a simply cut little black dress. "If you knew that, why didn't you buy that flashy red silk outfit? You would have stood out."

"I'll get plenty of attention this weekend," Hillary responded quietly, inhaling the exotic mixture of scents worn by the seminar participants. "Maurice should be in the spotlight this evening."

"You'd think we were at a funeral instead of a party," Melody grumbled, looking around the hotel ballroom. "This isn't a very lively crowd, is it?"

"That's the hushed air of reverence." Hillary managed a half smile.

"You aren't your usual perky self, either."

Hillary determinedly added the other half to her smile. "Nerves."

"Did you drink all the herb tea I brewed for you?"

"You made gallons. I did my best." Hillary's tongue curled in remembrance.

Fifteen, then twenty minutes passed. Hillary circled the crowded room, speaking to as many of the hundreds of people as she could. The response had been beyond her most optimistic estimates. Not only was she going to break even, Scentsations was actually going to make money.

Not everyone was a perfumer. She'd had the extraordinary good luck to host the first appearance by Maurice St. Etienne since the merger was announced. The press was there. Department-store heads were there. Editors from *Vogue* and *Harper's Bazaar* magazines were there. Photographers were there.

Paul was not there.

"The harps are a nice touch." Melody reappeared at her side. "I kind of expected samples of Chantal. This would be a wonderful advertising opportunity."

"Don't be silly." Hillary accepted a glass of champagne she had no intention of drinking. "Advertising is too modern and crass for the House of St. Etienne."

Melody declined the champagne. "The House of St. Etienne doesn't exist anymore."

"True." Hillary imagined Paul's pain whenever she thought of St. Etienne's surrender. The fashion press had talked of nothing else. Caroline had blitzed the media with the Chantal launch, too. No wonder Paul hadn't wanted to face the seminar participants. He must have felt that he had let both her and his grandfather down. Obstinate man, she thought with a sad fondness. If only he'd returned her calls.

She scanned the room with its creamy peach-and-gold decor, so kind to women's complexions. The subdued light glinted off the champagne flutes and the music of the harps accompanied the refined murmurs of several languages.

It was better than she'd dreamed.

And worse than she'd expected.

Hillary had rehearsed various speeches for meeting Paul's grandfather. Would she see Paul's features in Maurice's face? Had Paul spoken of her? Could she manage to ask why he hadn't come without sounding too pathetic, without revealing her hurt?

"Hillary." Worry colored Melody's voice. "We've been waiting forty-five minutes. Do you know if Maurice has arrived at the hotel yet?"

Hillary nodded. "I was informed by very protective members of his entourage that he's resting. They're taking care of everything." She grasped Melody's arm and gestured toward the doors. "Including his grand entrance."

Framed in the doorway was a short elderly man. The murmurs hushed, then scattered applause broke out. Every pair of eyes in the room watched Maurice St. Etienne execute an elegant bow and extend his arms in response to the accolades.

Every pair of eyes but Hillary's. Hers shifted to the younger man at Maurice's side. The one who gently steered his grandfather into a thoughtfully placed chair.

Paul.

Darkness ringed her vision as Hillary fought off a wave of light-headedness. She stumbled against a round table and abandoned her champagne.

The crowd surged toward Maurice leaving Hillary gripping the table.

"Breathe slowly and stand up straight." She felt Melody's steadying arm. "You can survive this. I'll tell the caterers to begin serving hors d'oeuvres." Melody discreetly slipped away.

He was here. Why?

All these weeks she'd thought of Paul, had been reminded of him constantly. *Their* plans. *Their* seminar.

And then he'd given up and allowed the merger with Dominique, anyway. How had he convinced his grandfather to agree to it?

Hillary studied the two of them. Maurice, though he appeared frail from a distance, glowed with the attention he was receiving. He hardly seemed the bitter and regret-filled man she'd expected him to be after the merger announcement. As she watched, Maurice threw back his head in a hearty laugh that carried across the room to her. He was happy, or at least doing an excellent job of pretending.

And Paul? His profile was to her and Hillary couldn't read his expression. How was he? Were those new lines of strain on his face?

At that instant Paul turned. Their gazes locked and he started walking toward her.

Hillary felt a lump forming in her throat with the usual bad timing such lumps had. She wanted to appear cool and unemotional, not frozen with nerves. She swallowed, but the lump remained.

Darn it, she'd thought she was all cried out.

And then Paul was there, standing in front of her.

"Hillary." He poured the syllables slowly, like honey. The way he had the first time he'd said her name.

She hadn't rehearsed any speeches for meeting Paul. So many questions... "Why?" she whispered at last, unable to trust her voice to say anything else.

"Later." He placed a finger on her lips and smiled. "Come. Meet my grandfather." He reached for her hand, lacing his fingers with hers.

She tried to take strength from his touch, fearing she would need it to endure the rest of the evening. The hand holding hers was strong, sure and confident. Everything she wasn't.

She was going to blow the introduction. She was going to appear gauche and provincial. She was going to blubber. Or babble. Or both.

Hillary counted on a few extra moments to compose herself as they negotiated through the crowd, but people let them pass, and before she was ready she stood in front of Maurice St. Etienne.

She tried to smile and failed. She tried to say something and managed only a swallow.

He struggled to his feet, gripping Paul's arm for support. Maurice wasn't much taller than she. He extended both his hands to her and Hillary grasped them, conscious that Paul had not spoken.

"My dear." Maurice raised her hands and kissed them, then favored her with a beaming smile that told her where Paul had inherited his.

Maurice's grip was strong and his brown eyes were lively. He was small, but hardly the frail old man Hillary had been expecting. She felt a tug as Maurice pulled her toward him and kissed her on both cheeks. "You will make my grandson happy, eh?" With a final squeeze, he freed her. "Now go. Talk." This was said with a stern look directed at Paul.

Hillary stepped back, aware that Paul had not introduced her, and that it wasn't necessary.

Pulse points beating wildly, she avoided Paul's eyes.

"He's been eager to meet you," Paul said, bending his head to hers. "We can have a longer visit with him later."

"Can we?" Her voice wobbled, but she hoped the crowd noise masked it.

Paul's hand in the hollow of her back urged her away from his grandfather's admirers. "Hillary, don't cry."

She hadn't been going to until she heard the concern in his voice. She blinked rapidly, following him blindly through the crowd.

"Here." He held out a folded white handkerchief.

That did it. He carried a handkerchief. There just
weren't that many men who carried handkerchiefs on the
odd chance a lady would need one. Paul was perfect—if
she ignored the glaring fact that he hadn't called her. But
she couldn't, which was why she needed the handkerchief.

He led her to the seating area outside the ballroom.
Hillary sat on a soft peach-colored love seat and tried to
dry her tears without ruining her makeup or staining the
pristine whiteness of the linen square. A group of people wandered past them into the foyer.

She cleared her throat. "I didn't expect you to come."

Paul sat beside her. "I wasn't sure you'd want me to
come after you heard the news."

"Yes." Hillary bounced back. "I got the announcement." She finally looked at him. "Haven't been able to
dash out for my sample of Chantal yet."

Paul winced. "Are you terribly disappointed that we
didn't join forces and defeat the evil Dominique?"

"Terribly hurt. About that and the fact that you
walked out of my life."

They stared at each other until Hillary bent her head.
Paul spoke first. "I guess I felt the same way."

"Because I kept my appointment with Dominique after you *forbade* it?" she asked, meeting his eyes again.
"What did you expect me to do?"

A smile raised one corner of his mouth. "Keep your
appointment with Dominique."

Hillary ignored his attempt to lighten the mood. "All
I did was talk to them. You didn't even wait to hear what
happened. You left so fast there were skid marks."

"I was angry."

"So was I."

Paul stretched his legs in front of him and examined his shoes. "If I'd said please, would it have made a difference?"

Hillary replayed the conversation in her mind. "'Please' and 'forbid' aren't generally used in the same sentence."

"Ah." Paul nodded. "Grandfather was right. He tells me I am, on occasion, a touch arrogant."

"The very word I would have chosen."

He smiled ruefully. "When you wrote that you hadn't signed with Dominique, I thought that I might have been the reason."

"You were! They only wanted to buy my perfumes because they thought you were interested in them." Would it never stop hurting when she remembered that disastrous afternoon with Caroline Waite? Hillary twisted the handkerchief in her lap. Linen wrinkled so easily. She stared at the creases as they absorbed two great teardrops.

Paul's fingers tilted her chin until she looked at him. "Dominique wanted to buy your perfumes because they're good. I believe that, Hillary, just as I believe in you and your talent."

"I waited so long, but you didn't call!" Her voice rose in a wail, an unsophisticated wail.

Paul opened his arms and drew her close. "I did need the time, Hillary. So many people have walked out of my life. In you, I thought I'd found love and a partner—a companion. Someone to be with me, on my side, no matter what."

"It works both ways, you know."

"I realize that now. When I arrived back in France, Grandfather guessed something was wrong. I told him about you and our argument. And he told me I can't dictate people's feelings or put conditions on love. That was what he'd tried to do with Chantal and he lost her."

"Did you also tell him about Dominique?"

Paul nodded.

"And he agreed to the merger."

"Just like that," Paul said quietly. "You were right. I shouldn't have tried to protect him by keeping him in ignorance. He thought Chantal had thrown away the perfume formula long ago. He was thrilled that the papers had been discovered and that once again, he could launch a new perfume." Paul took a deep breath before admitting, "That possibility had never occurred to me."

"A lot of things never occurred to you," Hillary grumbled. "Like letting me know you were coming."

Paul stroked her cheek. "But I promised you I'd come."

"You wrote that you would let me know your decision."

"About Dominique. You'd been able to decide quickly—I said I needed more time."

"But then—" Hillary struggled to recall Paul's second note "—you wrote that 'under the circumstances' you couldn't represent..." Hillary trailed off as Paul's meaning at last became clear.

"Ah, yes." Paul closed his eyes a moment. "I see how you could misinterpret my note. I thought you would have heard of the merger. News spread quickly."

"I haven't read the papers regularly in the past few months," Hillary admitted.

"I wrote that I couldn't be the representative because I have no position with the new company."

"What?" Hillary asked, stunned by Paul's revelation. "Who's in charge? Caroline?"

Paul shrugged. "I'm sure she'll be a member of the management team. As will my grandfather."

"How could you let them force you out?"

Paul looked surprised. "I asked to leave."

"Why?" Hillary had pushed away from him so she could look at his face. There *were* new lines. Fatigue...sadness.

He kissed her hair lightly. "I wouldn't have had any time for you."

Hillary's heart began a hopeful flutter.

"I've spent weeks facilitating a smooth conversion to the Dominique communications system, which is far superior to ours. I finished installing the computers and software in the last of our boutiques only a few days ago." He chuckled. "Do you know that I flew from Montreal to Paris just to escort my grandfather here? I haven't slept in who knows how long, and I haven't been to my office in two months."

"You always were bad about checking your messages."

He inhaled deeply. "And now I don't have to."

He closed his eyes and Hillary thought she saw him sway. "Paul, you're exhausted!" She brushed the hair back from his forehead. Was he a bit feverish?

He took her hand and kissed the palm before releasing it. When he looked at her, she saw that his eyes were red-rimmed. "I'm fine."

"You're not fine!"

Paul closed his eyes again before smiling lopsidedly. "Nothing a few weeks of sleep won't cure." As she watched, his face flushed, then whitened.

He didn't look well and hadn't for several minutes. "Paul." Hillary touched his hand. It was like ice. "Have you eaten anything?"

"Not lately." She watched in horror as he stood, then sank to the floor, one knee propped up. He was about to faint and she'd been badgering him about why he hadn't called. "Paul, it's okay. But when you didn't call—"

"Hillary."

"—I didn't think I'd ever see you again and I knew I'd been so stupid not to drop everything and come to France with you, but I thought I knew what was important to me, but I didn't—"

"Hillary," he repeated, capturing her hands, which had been flitting about wildly.

Hillary clung to him and frantically searched the foyer for help. "Put your head between your knees," she instructed, deepening her voice so it would sound calm and matter-of-fact.

"No!" He began to laugh.

Hysteria. "Paul, you have to!"

"Then I won't be able to see your face when I ask you to be my wife."

"What?"

He stared at her intently. "It was worth it. I wouldn't have missed that expression for anything."

"You're not sick?" Hillary started to realize that she was in the middle of a marriage proposal and not a medical emergency.

Paul's face had returned to its normal color. "Of sound mind and exhausted body." He looked at her quizzically. "And a touch nervous, perhaps?"

"You want to marry me?"

"More than anything. I love you, Hillary."

"I didn't think I'd ever hear you say that again." Hillary dabbed at her eyes with the soggy linen.

"No more tears." Paul sat back down and cupped her face with his hands. "I know how you feel about your perfumes, but I don't know how you feel about me." He searched her face, seeking an answer, then bent his head to hers.

All the feelings Hillary had tried so hard to bury in work were unearthed by Paul's kiss. It was a kiss filled with tenderness and healing. It promised new beginnings as it echoed happier times.

The sodden handkerchief dropped to the floor as Hillary clung to him, reveling in his familiar taste and scent.

"Well?"

Hillary could only stare at Paul, the man she'd thought she'd lost.

"You're trembling," he whispered, caressing her hair. "It's all right. I'm trembling, too."

He was. She could feel the thunderous pounding of his heart beneath her fingertips.

"Why didn't you tell me what you were going through? Why didn't you share it with me?" she whispered.

Paul touched his forehead to hers. "I'm not used to sharing problems. But Dominique and St. Etienne—whatever they'll call the new company—need not concern us anymore. I didn't want to ask you to be a part of that life. I wanted to start a new one. With you."

"I want that, too." Her hands covered his. How could she ever have considered living without him?

"Then say yes." His smile grew, coaxing one from her.

"Yes."

"And be sure to tell my grandfather that I was on bended knee. He insisted."

Hillary blinked and gave Paul another tremulous smile just before his arms encircled her. "I love you so much, but I didn't realize it in time. I was afraid of losing my identity.''

"You might have," Paul acknowledged. "Instead—" he smiled "—I lost mine."

How could she be so insensitive? She hadn't given up anything. *Paul* had.

Something of what she felt must have shown on her face, because he said, "Don't worry, I have plans."

"Such as?" she asked, and held her breath.

"After all those years of working to preserve a relic, I'm ready to start from scratch. I have long been aware that unknown designers have no display vehicle for their clothes. I've always wanted to support them."

"You mean open a boutique featuring their designs?"

"Yes, but even more. I want to promote their clothes. Give them a place to hold fashion shows."

Hillary grabbed his arm. "I know just the place. Earth Scents, or what was Earth Scents. Melody moved—I'll tell you all about that later. Anyway, she's been using the Earth Scents building as a warehouse. She hasn't had time to do anything with it yet. But Paul, the location would be perfect. Earth Scents is near a restored area of shops and restaurants that draws the university and museum crowd. There's no reason people couldn't drive a few more blocks. And there's a loft upstairs!"

"So it's bigger than your crystal closet?"

Hillary nodded excitedly. "It would be perfect for fashion shows. We could hold one a month—"

His laughter interrupted her. "I've missed you, Hillary."

She squeezed his hand. "I've missed you, too, but I'm in the middle of an idea.... Paul! We'll call it the Crystal Closet! Big windows running two stories...lots of glass so people can see the clothing displays...and I can design a fragrance for each collection!''

"I will insist that you design a fragrance for each collection. I intend this to be a showcase of your talents, as well."

Hillary arched an eyebrow at him. "Will we be in direct competition with Dominique-St. Etienne?"

"Most assuredly."

Hillary thought of Caroline and grinned. "I can't wait."

"Can Scentsations spare Natasha, do you think?" Paul asked as he stood up and offered his hand to a bubbling Hillary. "She'd be ideal to ferret out designers."

"She would. Oh, Paul, it'll be perfect!" Hillary threw out her arms and spun around. "Let's drive out there right after the reception!"

Paul shook his head. "I can't possibly keep up with you until I've had some sleep."

Hillary was immediately contrite. "I got carried away."

"Don't ever stop." Paul held her once more, his kiss making her dizzier than her spin.

"Don't you, either," she said.

"I believe in short engagements. Very short," Paul warned, disentangling her arms from around his neck. "Let's go back to the reception." He held out his hand and she slipped hers into it. "We have a merger of our own to announce."

HARLEQUIN

Romance

A Christmas tradition...

Imagine spending Christmas in New
Orleans with a blind stranger and his aged
guide dog—when you're supposed to be
there on your honeymoon!
#3163 Every Kind of Heaven
by Bethany Campbell

Imagine spending Christmas with a man
you once "married"—in a mock ceremony
at the age of eight!
#3166 The Forgetful Bride
by Debbie Macomber

*Available in December 1991, wherever
Harlequin books are sold.*

RXM

"INDULGE A LITTLE" SWEEPSTAKES

HERE'S HOW THE SWEEPSTAKES WORKS

NO PURCHASE NECESSARY

To enter each drawing, complete the appropriate Official Entry Form or a 3" by 5" index card by hand-printing your name, address and phone number and the trip destination that the entry is being submitted for (i.e., Walt Disney World Vacation Drawing, etc.) and mailing it to: Indulge '91 Subscribers-Only Sweepstakes, P.O. Box 1397, Buffalo, New York 14269-1397.

No responsibility is assumed for lost, late or misdirected mail. Entries must be sent separately with first class postage affixed, and be received by: 9/30/91 for the Walt Disney World Vacation Drawing, 10/31/91 for the Alaskan Cruise Drawing and 11/30/91 for the Hawaiian Vacation Drawing. Sweepstakes is open to residents of the U.S. and Canada, 21 years of age or older as of 11/7/91.

For complete rules, send a self-addressed, stamped (WA residents need not affix return postage) envelope to: Indulge '91 Subscribers-Only Sweepstakes Rules, P.O. Box 4005, Blair, NE 68009.

DIR-RL

"INDULGE A LITTLE" SWEEPSTAKES

HERE'S HOW THE SWEEPSTAKES WORKS

NO PURCHASE NECESSARY

To enter each drawing, complete the appropriate Official Entry Form or a 3" by 5" index card by hand-printing your name, address and phone number and the trip destination that the entry is being submitted for (i.e., Walt Disney World Vacation Drawing, etc.) and mailing it to: Indulge '91 Subscribers-Only Sweepstakes, P.O. Box 1397, Buffalo, New York 14269-1397.

No responsibility is assumed for lost, late or misdirected mail. Entries must be sent separately with first class postage affixed, and be received by: 9/30/91 for the Walt Disney World Vacation Drawing, 10/31/91 for the Alaskan Cruise Drawing and 11/30/91 for the Hawaiian Vacation Drawing. Sweepstakes is open to residents of the U.S. and Canada, 21 years of age or older as of 11/7/91.

For complete rules, send a self-addressed, stamped (WA residents need not affix return postage) envelope to: Indulge '91 Subscribers-Only Sweepstakes Rules, P.O. Box 4005, Blair, NE 68009.

© 1991 HARLEQUIN ENTERPRISES LTD.   DIR-RL

INDULGE A LITTLE—WIN A LOT!

Summer of '91 Subscribers-Only Sweepstakes

OFFICIAL ENTRY FORM

This entry must be received by: Oct. 31, 1991
This month's winner will be notified by: Nov. 7, 1991
Trip must be taken between: May 27, 1992—Sept. 9, 1992
(depending on sailing schedule)

YES, I want to win the Alaska Cruise vacation for two. I understand the prize includes round-trip airfare, one-week cruise including private cabin, all meals and pocket money as revealed on the "wallet" scratch-off card.

Name _____

Address_____ Apt. _____

City _____

State/Prov. _____ Zip/Postal Code _____

Daytime phone number _____
                                    (Area Code)

Return entries with invoice in envelope provided. Each book in this shipment has two entry coupons—and the more coupons you enter, the better your chances of winning!

© 1991 HARLEQUIN ENTERPRISES LTD.   2N-CPS